HAPPINESS
and other stories

D1321252

HAPPINESS

and other stories
by Mary Lavin

CONSTABLE
LONDON

Published by Constable and Company Limited
10 Orange Street, London, WC2
Copyright © 1969 Mary Lavin
SBN 09 456540 6

These stories first appeared in
The New Yorker, Cosmopolitan, The Kenyon Review
and *The Southern Review*
Printed in Great Britain by The Anchor Press Ltd.,
and bound by Wm. Brendon & Son Ltd.,
both of Tiptree, Essex

For my daughters
Elizabeth and Caroline

Contents

Happiness

Mother had a lot to say. This does not mean she was always talking but that we children felt the wells she drew upon were deep, deep, deep. Her theme was happiness: what it was, what it was not; where we might find it, where not; and how, if found, it must be guarded. Never must we confound it with pleasure. Nor think sorrow its exact opposite.

'Take Father Hugh,' Mother's eyes flashed as she looked at him. 'According to him, sorrow is an ingredient of happiness – a *necessary* ingredient, if you please!' And when he tried to protest she put up her hand. 'There may be a freakish truth in the theory – for some people. But not for me. And not, I hope, for my children.' She looked severely at us three girls. We laughed. None of us had had much experience with sorrow. Bea and I were children and Linda only a year old when our father died suddenly after a short illness that had not at first seemed serious. 'I've known people to make sorrow a *substitute* for happiness,' Mother said.

Father Hugh protested again. 'You're not putting me in that class, I hope?'

Father Hugh, ever since our father died, had been

the closest of anyone to us as a family, without being close to any one of us in particular – even to Mother. He lived in a monastery near our farm in County Meath, and he had been one of the celebrants at the Requiem High Mass our father's political importance had demanded. He met us that day for the first time, but he took to dropping in to see us, with the idea of filling the crater of loneliness left at our centre. He did not know that there was a cavity in his own life, much less that we would fill it. He and Mother were both young in those days, and perhaps it gave scandal to some that he was so often in our house, staying till late into the night and, indeed, thinking nothing of stopping all night if there was any special reason, such as one of us being sick. He had even on occasion slept there if the night was too wet for tramping home across the fields.

When we girls were young, we were so used to having Father Hugh around that we never stood on ceremony with him but in his presence dried our hair and pared our nails and never minded what garments were strewn about. As for Mother – she thought nothing of running out of the bathroom in her slip, brushing her teeth or combing her hair, if she wanted to tell him something she might otherwise forget. And she brooked no criticism of her behaviour. 'Celibacy was never meant to take all the warmth and homeliness out of their lives,' she said.

On this point, too, Bea was adamant. Bea, the middle sister, was our oracle. 'I'm so glad he *has* Mother,' she said, 'as well as her having him, because it must be awful the way most women treat them – priests, I mean – as if they were pariahs. Mother treats him like a human being – that's all!'

And when it came to Mother's ears that there had been gossip about her making free with Father Hugh, she opened her eyes wide in astonishment. 'But he's only a priest!' she said.

Bea giggled. 'It's a good job he didn't hear *that*,' she said to me afterwards. 'It would undo the good she's done him. You'd think he was a eunuch.'

'Bea!' I said. 'Do you think he's in love with her?'

'If so, he doesn't know it,' Bea said firmly. 'It's her soul he's after! Maybe he wants to make sure of her in the next world!'

But thoughts of the world to come never troubled Mother. 'If anything ever happens to me, children,' she said, 'suddenly, I mean, or when you are not near me, or I cannot speak to you, I want you to promise you won't feel bad. There's no need! Just remember that I had a happy life – and that if I had to choose my kind of heaven I'd take it on this earth with you again, no matter how much you might annoy me!'

You see, annoyance and fatigue, according to Mother, and even illness and pain, could coexist with happiness. She had a habit of asking people if they were happy at times and in places that – to say the least of it – seemed to us inappropriate. 'But are you happy?' she'd probe as one lay sick and bathed in sweat, or in the throes of a jumping toothache. And once in our presence she made the inquiry of an old friend as he lay upon his deathbed.

'Why not?' she said when we took her to task for it later. 'Isn't it more important than ever to be happy when you're dying? Take my own father! You know what he said in his last moments? On his deathbed, he defied me to name a man who had enjoyed a better life. In spite of dreadful pain, his face *radiated* happiness!' Mother nodded her head comfortably. 'Happiness drives out pain, as fire burns out fire.'

Having no knowledge of our own to pit against hers, we thirstily drank in her rhetoric. Only Bea was sceptical. 'Perhaps you *got* it from him, like spots, or fever,' she said. 'Or something that could at least be slipped from hand to hand.'

'Do you think I'd have taken it if that were the case!' Mother cried. 'Then, when he needed it most?'

'Not there and then!' Bea said stubbornly. 'I meant as a sort of legacy.'

'Don't you think in *that* case,' Mother said, exasperated, 'he would have felt obliged to leave it to your grandmother?'

Certainly we knew that in spite of his lavish heart our grandfather had failed to provide our grandmother with enduring happiness. He had passed that job on to Mother. And Mother had not made too good a fist of it, even when Father was living and she had him — and, later, us children — to help.

As for Father Hugh, he had given our grandmother up early in the game. 'God Almighty couldn't make that woman happy,' he said one day, seeing Mother's face, drawn and pale with fatigue, preparing for the nightly run over to her own mother's flat that would exhaust her utterly.

There were evenings after she came home from the library where she worked when we saw her stand with the car keys in her hand, trying to think which would be worse – to slog over there on foot, or take out the car again. And yet the distance was short. It was Mother's day that had been too long.

'Weren't you over to see her this morning?' Father Hugh demanded.

'No matter!' said Mother. She was no doubt thinking of the forlorn face our grandmother always put on when she was leaving. ('Don't say good night, Vera,' Grandmother would plead. 'It makes me feel too lonely. And you never can tell – you might slip over again before you go to bed!')

'Do you know the time?' Bea would say impatiently, if she happened to be with Mother. Not indeed that the lateness of the hour counted for anything, because in all likelihood Mother *would* go back, if only to pass by under the window and see that the lights were out, or stand and listen and make sure that as far as she could tell all was well.

'I wouldn't mind if she was happy,' Mother said.

'And how do you know she's not?' we'd ask.

'When people are happy, I can feel it. Can't you?'

We were not sure. Most people thought our grandmother was a gay creature, a small birdy being who

B

even at a great age laughed like a girl, and – more remarkably – sang like one, as she went about her day. But beak and claw were of steel. She'd think nothing of sending Mother back to a shop three times if her errands were not exactly right. 'Not sugar like that – that's *too* fine; it's not castor sugar I want. But *not* as coarse as *that*, either. I want an in-between kind.'

Provoked one day, my youngest sister, Linda, turned and gave battle. 'You're mean!' she cried. 'You love ordering people about!'

Grandmother preened, as if Linda had acclaimed an attribute. 'I was always hard to please,' she said. 'As a girl, I used to be called Miss Imperious.'

And Miss Imperious she remained as long as she lived, even when she was a great age. Her orders were then given a wry twist by the fact that as she advanced in age she took to calling her daughter Mother, as we did.

There was one great phrase with which our grandmother opened every sentence: 'if only'. 'If only,' she'd say, when we came to visit her – 'if only you'd come earlier, before I was worn out expecting you!' Or if we were early, then if only it was later, after she'd had a rest and could enjoy us, be *able* for us. And if we brought her flowers, she'd sigh to think that if only we'd brought them the previous day she'd have had a visitor to appreciate them, or say it was a pity the stems weren't longer. If only we'd picked a few green leaves, or included some buds, because, she said disparagingly, the poor flowers we'd brought were already wilting. We might just as well not have brought them! As the years went on, Grandmother had a new bead to add to her rosary: if only her friends were not all dead! By their absence, they reduced to nil all *real* enjoyment in anything. Our own father – her son-in-law – was the one person who had ever gone close to pleasing her. But even here there had been a snag. 'If only he was my real son!' she used to say, with a sigh.

Mother's mother lived on through our childhood and into our early maturity (though she outlived the money our grandfather left her), and in our minds she was a complicated mixture of valiance and defeat. Courageous and generous within the limits of her own life, her simplest demand was yet enormous in the larger frame of Mother's life, and so we never could see her with the same clarity of vision with which we saw our grandfather, or our own father. Them we saw only through Mother's eyes.

'Take your grandfather!' she'd cry, and instantly we'd see him, his eyes burning upon us – yes, upon *us*, although in his day only one of us had been born: me. At another time, Mother would cry, 'Take your own father!' and instantly we'd see *him* – tall, handsome, young, and much more suited to marry one of us than poor bedraggled Mother.

Most fascinating of all were the times Mother would say 'Take me!' By magic then, staring down the years, we'd see blazingly clear a small girl with black hair and buttoned boots, who, though plain and pouting,

burned bright, like a star. 'I was happy, you see,'
Mother said. And we'd strain hard to try and understand the mystery of the light that still radiated from
her. 'I used to lean along a tree that grew out over the
river,' she said, 'and look down through the grey
leaves at the water flowing past below, and I used to
think it was not the stream that flowed but me, spread-
eagled over it, who flew through the air! Like a bird!
That I'd found the secret!' She made it seem there
might *be* such a secret, just waiting to be found.
Another time she'd dream that she'd be a great singer.

'We didn't know you sang, Mother!'

She had to laugh. 'Like a crow,' she said.

Sometimes she used to think she'd swim the
Channel.

'Did you swim *that* well, Mother?'

'Oh, not really — just the breast stroke,' she said.
'And then only by the aid of two pig bladders blown
up by my father and tied around my middle. But I used
to throb — yes, throb — with happiness.'

Behind Mother's back, Bea raised her eyebrows.

What was it, we used to ask ourselves — that quality
that she, we felt sure, misnamed? Was it courage?
Was it strength, health, or high spirits? Something you
could not give or take — a conundrum? A game of
catch-as-catch-can?

'I know,' cried Bea. 'A sham!'

Whatever it was, we knew that Mother would let no
wind of violence from within or without tear it from
her. Although, one evening when Father Hugh was

with us, our astonished ears heard her proclaim that there might be a time when one had to slacken hold on it – let go – to catch at it again with a surer hand. In the way, we supposed, that the high-wire walker up among the painted stars of his canvas sky must wait to fling himself through the air until the bar he catches at has started to sway perversely from him. Oh no, no! That downward drag at our innards we could not bear, the belly swelling to the shape of a pear. Let happiness go by the board. 'After all, lots of people seem to make out without it,' Bea cried. It was too tricky a business. And might it not be that one had to be born with a flair for it?

'A flair would not be enough,' Mother answered. 'Take Father Hugh. He, if anyone, had a flair for it – a natural capacity! You've only to look at him when he's off guard, with you children, or helping me in the garden. But he rejects happiness! He casts it from him.'

'That is simply not true, Vera,' cried Father Hugh, overhearing her. 'It's just that I don't place an inordinate value on it like you. I don't think it's enough to carry one all the way. To the end, I mean – and after.'

'Oh, don't talk about the end when we're only in the middle,' cried Mother. And, indeed, at that moment her own face shone with such happiness it was hard to believe that her earth was not her heaven. Certainly it was her constant contention that of happiness she had had a lion's share. This, however, we, in private, doubted. Perhaps there were times when she had had a surplus of it — when she was young, say, with her redoubtable father, whose love blazed circles around her, making winter into summer and ice into fire. Perhaps she did have a brimming measure in her early married years. By straining hard, we could find traces left in our minds from those days of milk and honey. Our father, while he lived, had cast a magic over everything, for us as well as for her. He held his love up over us like an umbrella and kept off the troubles that afterwards came down on us, pouring cats and dogs!

But if she did have more than the common lot of happiness in those early days, what use was that when we could remember so clearly how our father's death had ravaged her? And how could we forget the distress it brought on us when, afraid to let her out of our sight, Bea and I stumbled after her everywhere, through the woods and along the bank of the river, where, in the weeks that followed, she tried vainly to find peace.

The summer after Father died, we were invited to France to stay with friends, and when she went walking on the cliffs at Fécamp our fears for her grew frenzied, so that we hung on to her arm and dragged at her skirt, hoping that like leaded weights we'd pin her down if she went too near to the edge. But at night we had to abandon our watch, being forced to follow the conventions of a family still whole — a home still intact — and go to bed at the same time as the other children. It was at that hour, when the coast guard

was gone from his rowing boat offshore and the sand
was as cold and grey as the sea, that Mother liked to
swim. And when she had washed, kissed, and left us,
our hearts almost died inside us and we'd creep out of
bed again to stand in our bare feet at the mansard and
watch as she ran down the shingle, striking out when
she reached the water where, far out, wave and sky and
mist were one, and the greyness closed over her. If we
took our eyes off her for an instant, it was impossible
to find her again.

'Oh, make her turn back, God, please!' I prayed out
loud one night.

Startled, Bea turned away from the window. 'She'll
have to turn back sometime, won't she? Unless . . .?'

Locking our damp hands together, we stared out
again. 'She wouldn't!' I whispered. 'It would be a
sin!'

Secure in the deterring power of sin, we let out our
breath. Then Bea's breath caught again. 'What if she
went out so far she used up all her strength? She
couldn't swim back! It wouldn't be a sin then!'

'It's the intention that counts,' I whispered.

A second later, we could see an arm lift heavily up
and wearily cleave down, and at last Mother was in the
shallows, wading back to shore.

'Don't let her see us!' cried Bea. As if our chattering
teeth would not give us away when she looked in at us
before she went to her own room on the other side of
the corridor, where, later in the night, sometimes the
sound of crying would reach us.

What was it worth – a happiness bought that
dearly.

Mother had never questioned it. And once she told
us, 'On a wintry day, I brought my own mother a snowdrop. It was the first one of the year – a bleak bud that
had come up stunted before its time – and I meant it
for a sign. But do you know what your grandmother
said? "What good are snowdrops to me now?" Such
a thing to say! What good is a snowdrop at all if it
doesn't hold its value always, and never lose it! Isn't
that the whole point of a snowdrop? And that is the
whole point of happiness, too! What good would it be
if it could be erased without trace? Take me and those
daffodils!' Stooping, she buried her face in a bunch
that lay on the table waiting to be put in vases. 'If they
didn't hold their beauty absolute and inviolable, do
you think I could bear the sight of them after what
happened when your father was in hospital?'

It was a fair question. When Father went to hospital,
Mother went with him and stayed in a small hotel
across the street so she could be with him all day from
early to late. 'Because it was so awful for him–being in
Dublin!' she said. 'You have no idea how he hated it.'

That he was dying neither of them realised. How
could they know, as it rushed through the sky, that
their star was a falling star! But one evening when
she'd left him asleep Mother came home for a few
hours to see how we were faring, and it broke her
heart to see the daffodils out all over the place – in the

woods, under the trees, and along the sides of the avenue. There had never been so many, and she thought how awful it was that Father was missing them. 'You sent up little bunches to him, you poor dears!' she said. 'Sweet little bunches, too – squeezed tight as posies by your little fists! But stuffed into vases they couldn't really make up to him for not being able to see them growing!'

So on the way back to the hospital she stopped her car and pulled a great bunch – the full of her arms. 'They took up the whole back seat,' she said, 'and I was so excited at the thought of walking into his room and dumping them on his bed – you know – just plomping them down so he could smell them, and feel them, and look and look! I didn't mean them to be put in vases, or anything ridiculous like that – it would have taken a rainwater barrel to hold them. Why, I could hardly see over them as I came up the steps; I kept tripping. But when I came into the hall, that nun – I told you about her – that nun came up to me, sprang out of nowhere it seemed, although I know now that she was waiting for me, knowing that somebody had to bring me to my senses. But the way she did it! Reached out and grabbed the flowers, letting lots of them fall – I remember them getting stood on. 'Where are you going with those foolish flowers, you foolish woman?' she said. 'Don't you know your husband is dying? Your prayers are all you can give him now!'

'She was right. I *was* foolish. But I wasn't cured.

Afterwards, it was nothing but foolishness the way I dragged you children after me all over Europe. As if any one place was going to be different from another, any better, any less desolate. But there was great satisfaction in bringing you places your father and I had planned to bring you – although in fairness to him I must say that he would not perhaps have brought you so young. And he would not have had an ulterior motive. But above all, he would not have attempted those trips in such a dilapidated car.'

Oh, that car! It was a battered and dilapidated red sports car, so depleted of accessories that when, eventually, we got a new car Mother still stuck out her hand on bends, and in wet weather jumped out to wipe the windscreen with her sleeve. And if fussed, she'd let down the window and shout at people, forgetting she now had a horn. How we had ever fitted into it with all our luggage was a miracle.

'You were never lumpish – any of you!' Mother said proudly. 'But you were very healthy and very strong.' She turned to me. 'Think of how you got that car up the hill in Switzerland!'

'The Alps are not hills, Mother!' I pointed out coldly, as I had done at the time, when, as actually happened, the car failed to make it on one of the inclines. Mother let it run back until it wedged against the rock face, and I had to get out and push till she got going again in first gear. But when it got started it couldn't be stopped to pick me up until it got to the top, where they had to wait for me, and for a very long time.

'Ah, well,' she said, sighing wistfully at the thought of those trips. 'You got something out of them, I hope. All that travelling must have helped you with your geography and your history.'

We looked at each other and smiled, and then Mother herself laughed. 'Remember the time,' she said, 'when we were in Italy, and it was Easter, and all the shops were chock-full of food? The butchers' shops had poultry and game hanging up outside the doors, fully feathered, and with their poor heads dripping blood, and in the windows they had poor little lambs and suckling pigs and young goats, all skinned and hanging by their hindfeet.' Mother shuddered. 'They think so much about food. I found it revolting. I had to hurry past. But Linda, who must have been only four then, dragged at me and stared and stared. You know how children are at that age; they have a morbid fascination for what is cruel and bloody. Her face was flushed and her eyes were wide. I hurried her back to the hotel. But next morning she crept into my room. She crept up to me and pressed against me. "Can't we go back, just once, and look again at that shop?" she whispered. "The shop where they have the little children hanging up for Easter!" It was the young goats, of course, but I'd said "kids", I suppose. How we laughed.' But her face was grave. 'You were *so* good on those trips, all of you,' she said. 'You were really very good children in general. Otherwise I would never have put so much effort into rearing you, because I wasn't a bit maternal. You brought out the best in me! I put an unnatural effort into you, of course, because I was taking my standards from your father, forgetting that his might not have remained so inflexible if he had lived to middle age and was beset by life, like other parents.'

'Well, the job is nearly over now, Vera,' said Father Hugh. 'And you didn't do so badly.'

'That's right, Hugh,' said Mother, and she straightened up, and put her hand to her back the way she sometimes did in the garden when she got up from her knees after weeding. 'I didn't go over to the enemy anyway! We survived!' Then a flash of defiance came into her eyes. 'And we were happy. That's the main thing!'

Father Hugh frowned. 'There you go again!' he said.

Mother turned on him. 'I don't think you realise the onslaughts that were made upon our happiness! The minute Robert died, they came down on me – cohorts of relatives, friends, even strangers, all draped in black, opening their arms like bats to let me pass into their company. "Life is a vale of tears," they said. "You are privileged to find it out so young!" Ugh! After I staggered on to my feet and began to take hold of life once more, they fell back defeated. And the first day I gave a laugh – pouff, they were blown out like candles. They weren't living in a real world at all; they belonged to a ghostly world where life was easy: all one had to do was sit and weep. It takes effort to push back the stone from the mouth of the tomb and walk out.'

Effort. Effort. Ah, but that strange-sounding word could invoke little sympathy from those who had not learned yet what it meant. Life must have been hardest for Mother in those years when we older ones were at college – no longer children, and still dependent on her. Indeed, we made more demands on her than ever then, having moved into new areas of activity and emotion. And our friends! Our friends came and went as freely as we did ourselves, so that the house was often like a café – and one where pets were not prohibited but took their places on our chairs and beds, as regardless as the people. And anyway it was hard to have sympathy for someone who got things into such a state as Mother. All over the house there was clutter. Her study was like the returned-letter department of a post-office, with stacks of paper everywhere, bills paid and unpaid, letters answered and unanswered, tax returns, pamphlets, leaflets. If by mistake we left the door open on a windy day, we came back to find papers flapping through the air like frightened birds. Efficient only in that she managed eventually to conclude every task she began, it never seemed possible to outsiders that by Mother's methods anything whatever could be accomplished. In an attempt to keep order elsewhere, she made her own room the clearing house into which the rest of us put everything: things to be given away, things to be mended, things to be stored, things to be treasured, things to be returned – even things to be thrown out! By the end of the year, the room resembled an obsolescence dump. And no one could help her; the chaos of her life was as personal as an act of creation – one might as well try to finish another person's poem.

As the years passed, Mother rushed around more hectically. And although Bea and I had married and were not at home any more, except at holiday time and for occasional weekends, Linda was noisier than the two of us put together had been, and for every follower we had brought home she brought twenty. The house was never still. Now that we were reduced to being visitors, we watched Mother's tension mount to vertigo, knowing that, like a spinning top, she could not rest till she fell. But now at the smallest pretext Father Hugh would call in the doctor and Mother would be put on the mail boat and dispatched for London. For it was essential that she get far enough away to make phoning home every night prohibitively costly.

Unfortunately, the thought of departure often drove a spur into her and she redoubled her effort to achieve order in her affairs. She would be up until the early hours ransacking her desk. To her, as always the shortest parting entailed a preparation as for death. And as if it were her end that was at hand, we would all be summoned, although she had no time to speak a word to us, because five minutes before departure she would still be attempting to reply to letters that were the acquisition of weeks and would have taken whole days to dispatch.

'Don't you know the taxi is at the door, Vera?'

Father Hugh would say, running his hand through his grey hair and looking very dishevelled himself. She had him at times as distracted as herself. 'You can't do any more. You'll have to leave the rest till you come back.'

'I can't, I can't!' Mother would cry. 'I'll have to cancel my plans.'

One day, Father Hugh opened the lid of her case, which was strapped up in the hall, and with a swipe of his arm he cleared all the papers on the top of the desk pell-mell into the suitcase. 'You can sort them on the boat,' he said, 'or the train to London!'

Thereafter, Mother's luggage always included an empty case to hold the unfinished papers on her desk. And years afterwards a steward on the Irish Mail told us she was a familiar figure, working away at letters and bills nearly all the way from Holyhead to Euston. 'She gave it up about Rugby or Crewe,' he said. 'She'd get talking to someone in the compartment.' He smiled. 'There was one time coming down the train I was just in time to see her close up the window with a guilty look. I didn't say anything, but I think she'd emptied those papers of hers out the window!'

Quite likely. When we were children, even a few hours away from us gave her composure. And in two weeks or less, when she'd come home, the well of her spirit would be freshened. We'd hardly know her – her step so light, her eye so bright, and her love and patience once more freely flowing. But in no time at all the house would fill up once more with the noise and confusion of too many people and too many animals, and again we'd be fighting our corner with cats and dogs, bats, mice, bees and even wasps. 'Don't kill it!' Mother would cry if we raised a hand to an angry wasp. 'Just catch it, dear, and put it outside. Open the window and let it fly away!' But even this treatment could at times be deemed too harsh. 'Wait a minute. Close the window!' she'd cry. 'It's too cold outside. It will die. That's why it came in, I suppose! Oh dear, what will we do?' Life would be going full blast again.

There was only one place Mother found rest. When she was at breaking point and fit to fall, she'd go out into the garden – not to sit or stroll around but to dig, to drag up weeds, to move great clumps of corms or rhizomes, or indeed quite frequently to haul huge rocks from one place to another. She was always laying down a path, building a dry wall, or making compost heaps as high as hills. However jaded she might be going out, when dark forced her in at last her step had the spring of a daisy. So if she did not succeed in defining happiness to our understanding, we could see that whatever it was, she possessed it to the full when she was in her garden.

One of us said as much one Sunday when Bea and I had dropped round for the afternoon. Father Hugh was with us again. 'It's an unthinking happiness, though,' he cavilled. We were standing at the drawing-room window, looking out to where in the fading light we could see Mother on her knees weeding, in the long border that stretched from the house right down to the woods. 'I wonder how she'd take it if she were stricken down and had to give up that heavy work!' he said. Was he perhaps a little jealous of how she could stoop and bend? He himself had begun to use a stick. I was often a little jealous of her myself, because although I was married and had children of my own, I had married young and felt the weight of living as heavy as a weight of years. 'She doesn't take enough care of herself,' Father Hugh said sadly. 'Look at her out there with nothing under her knees to protect her from the damp ground.' It was almost too dim for us to see her, but even in the drawing room it was chilly. 'She should not be let stay out there after the sun goes down.'

'Just you try to get her in then!' said Linda, who had come into the room in time to hear him. 'Don't you know by now anyway that what would kill another person only seems to make Mother thrive?'

Father Hugh shook his head again. 'You seem to forget it's not younger she's getting!' He fidgeted and fussed, and several times went to the window to stare out apprehensively. He was really getting quite elderly.

'Come and sit down, Father Hugh,' Bea said, and to take his mind off Mother she turned on the light and blotted out the garden. Instead of seeing through the window, we saw into it as into a mirror, and there between the flower-laden tables and the lamps it was ourselves we saw moving vaguely. Like Father Hugh,

C

we, too, were waiting for her to come in before we called an end to the day.

'Oh, this is ridiculous!' Father Hugh cried at last. 'She'll have to listen to reason.' And going back to the window he threw it open. 'Vera!' he called. 'Vera!' – sternly, so sternly that, more intimate than an endearment, his tone shocked us. 'She didn't hear me,' he said, turning back blinking at us in the lighted room. 'I'm going out to get her.' And in a minute he was gone from the room. As he ran down the garden path, we stared at each other, astonished; his step, like his voice, was the step of a lover. 'I'm coming, Vera!' he cried.

Although she was never stubborn except in things that mattered, Mother had not moved. In the wholehearted way she did everything, she was bent down close to the ground. It wasn't the light only that was dimming; her eyesight also was failing, I thought, as instinctively I followed Father Hugh.

But halfway down the path I stopped. I had seen something he had not: Mother's hand that appeared to support itself in a forked branch of an old tree peony she had planted as a bride was not in fact gripping it but impaled upon it. And the hand that appeared to be grubbing in the clay in fact was sunk into the soft mould. 'Mother!' I screamed, and I ran forward, but when I reached her I covered my face with my hands. 'Oh Father Hugh!' I cried. 'Is she dead?'

It was Bea who answered, hysterical. 'She is! She is!' she cried, and she began to pound Father Hugh on the back with her fists, as if his pessimistic words had made this happen.

But Mother was not dead. And at first the doctor even offered hope of her pulling through. But from the moment Father Hugh lifted her up to carry her into the house we ourselves had no hope, seeing how effortlessly he, who was not strong, could carry her. When he put her down on her bed, her head hardly creased the pillow. Mother lived for four more hours.

Like the days of her life, those four hours that Mother lived were packed tight with concern and anxiety. Partly conscious, partly delirious, she seemed to think the counterpane was her desk, and she scrabbled her fingers upon it as if trying to sort out a muddle of bills and correspondence. No longer indifferent now, we listened, anguished, to the distracted cries that had for all our lifetime been so familiar to us. 'Oh, where is it? Where is it? I had it a minute ago! Where on earth did I put it?'

'Vera, Vera, stop worrying,' Father Hugh pleaded, but she waved him away and went on sifting through the sheets as if they were sheets of paper. 'Oh, Vera!' he begged. 'Listen to me. Do you not know—'

Bea pushed between them. 'You're not to tell her!' she commanded. 'Why frighten her?'

'But it ought not to frighten her,' said Father Hugh. 'This is what I was always afraid would happen – that she'd be frightened when it came to the end.'

At that moment, as if to vindicate him, Mother's hands fell idle on the coverlet, palm upward and empty. And turning her head she stared at each of us in turn, beseechingly. 'I cannot face it,' she whispered. 'I can't! I can't! I can't!'

'Oh, my God!' Bea said, and she started to cry.

'Vera. For God's sake listen to me,' Father Hugh cried, and pressing his face to hers, as close as a kiss, he kept whispering to her, trying to cast into the dark tunnel before her the light of his own faith.

But it seemed to us that Mother must already be looking into God's exigent eyes. 'I can't!' she cried. 'I can't!'

Then her mind came back from the stark world of the spirit to the world where her body was still detained, but even that world was now a whirling kaleidoscope of things which only she could see. Suddenly her eyes focussed, and, catching at Father Hugh, she pulled herself up a little and pointed to something we could not see. 'What will be done with them?' Her voice was anxious. 'They ought to be put in water anyway,' she said, and, leaning over the edge of the bed, she pointed to the floor. 'Don't step on that one!' she said sharply. Then, more sharply still, she addressed us all. 'Have them sent to the public ward,' she said peremptorily. 'Don't let that nun take them; she'll only put them on the altar. And God doesn't want them! He made them for *us* – not for Himself!'

It was the familiar rhetoric that all her life had characterised her utterances. For a moment we were mystified. Then Bea gasped. 'The daffodils!' she cried.

'The day Father died!' And over her face came the
light that had so often blazed over Mother's. Leaning
across the bed, she pushed Father Hugh aside. And,
putting out her hands, she held Mother's face between
her palms as tenderly as if it were the face of a child. 'It's
all right, Mother. You don't *have* to face it! It's over!'
Then she who had so fiercely forbade Father Hugh to do
so blurted out the truth. 'You've finished with this
world, Mother,' she said, and, confident that her
tidings were joyous, her voice was strong.

Mother made the last effort of her life and grasped
at Bea's meaning. She let out a sigh, and, closing her
eyes, she sank back, and this time her head sank so
deep into the pillow that it would have been dented
had it been a pillow of stone.

The New Gardener

Clem was the man for us. 'No matter. I'll get it to rights,' he said blithely, when he saw the state of the garden. Five weeks of early spring with no man in it, and a wet season at that, it was a fright. 'And now where's the cottage?' he asked.

He had crossed over from Holyhead on the night boat, come down to Bective on the bus and walked up from the crossroads. 'I left the family in Dublin,' he said. 'I want to get the cottage fixed up before they see it. It was a rough crossing, and Pearl got a little sick.'

Which was Pearl? The snapshots he'd sent in lieu of an interview had shown him surrounded by a nice-sized family for so young a man. Holding on to one arm was a woman, presumably his wife, but she must have stirred as the snap was being taken, because she was a bit blurred. Her dark hair was cloudy anyway and it partly hid her face. In spite of the blurring, her features looked sharp though, but this was of small moment as long as she could take care of the small children that clung about Clem, especially the baby girl, who snuggled in his arms.

'They're coming down on the evening bus,' he

explained. 'Where can I get a horse and cart? I want to pick up a few sticks of furniture for the place. I suppose I'll get one in the farmyard?'

In a few minutes he was rattling off in the farm cart, standing with his legs apart, his yellow hair lifting in the breeze of his departure, and the white tennis shoes – which he had worn also in the snap – looking, to the last glimpse, magnificently unsuitable. In less than an hour he was back with a load of fat mattresses, bulging pillows and bedding, the lot barricaded into the cart by a palisade of table legs and up-ended chairs.

'Another run and the job is done,' he cried, as he toppled it all out on the grass patch in front of the cottage, and galloped off to town once more.

The second time he could be heard coming a mile away with a load of ewers and basins, pots and several pans, wash-hand stands, an oil cooker and tin cans, that clattered together on the cart behind him. 'These must be got into the house at once,' he said solicitously to a young lad sent up from the yard to help him. 'There's damp in the air, and I don't want them rusted. Don't stand there gawking, boy,' he added, as Jimmy stared at the bedding already beaded with mist. 'Bedding is easy aired. Rust is a serious matter. Learn to distinguish!'

Then there began such a fury of lifting and carrying, pushing and pulling, such banging of nails and bringing down of plaster, but above all, such running in and out of the cottage that Clem's shoes came at

last into their own. They were so apt for the job
on foot.

By evening every picture was hung, every plate in
place, the tables and chairs were right side up and the
oil cooker lit and giving off its perfume. The bedding
was still outdoors.

'No matter. Food comes first. Learn to distinguish!'
cried Clem again, as he held a plate under a brown-
paper bag and let plop out a mess of cream buns.
'They'll be starving,' he said. 'Pearl isn't much of a
feeder,' he added sadly, 'but the others have powerful
appetites.'

He still hadn't said which was Pearl, but it wasn't
the wife anyway, because when Jimmy saw them
trudging up the drive a while later, there was no wife,
there was only Clem with the two small boys, the
bigger girl, and the little one in his arms snuggled
close to him, just as in the snap, with only her curls
to be seen. Yet when Clem let down the child, Jimmy
wondered no more, for she was the dead spit of a
pearl.

'Did you ever see the like of her?' cried Clem
delightedly, as he saw Jimmy looking at her. 'She puts
me in mind of apple blossom! That's what I should
have called her – Blossom,' he said sadly, 'but no
matter. I don't like fancy names anyway. Come now,
Moll!' he said, turning to the bigger girl, 'let's get
her to bed. She's dog-tired.' Planting Pearl in Moll's
arms, he ran out and pulled in one of the mattresses.
'It's a bit damp all right,' he said, in surprise. But,

undismayed, he dashed into the garden and came back
with three large rhubarb leaves. 'Put them under the
sheet,' he said. 'Leaves are waterproof. Trust nature
every time.' Then as Moll was about to stagger away
with Pearl in her arms, he ran after them and gave
Moll a hug. 'She's the best little mother in the world,'
he said. 'I don't know what I'd do without her.'

It was the first and last reference, oblique as it was,
to the absence of Mrs. Clem.

As the days went on, however, the absence of Mrs.
Clem was seldom felt, for if Clem was a good father,
he was a still better mother. True, he sometimes had
to knock off work in the garden to cook a hot meal
for them all, to fetch them from school, or oftenest
of all to wash Pearl's hair, but he still did more work
in one day than another man would in six. And it
wasn't just hard work: Clem had a green hand if ever
man had.

On the first morning of all, he made his only com-
plaint. 'There isn't enough shelter in this garden,' he
said. 'Living things are very tender.' And disregarding
the fact that he'd just whitened his tennis shoes, he
leaped into the soft black clay of the border and broke
off branches recklessly from syringa, philadelphus
and daphne. Then he rushed around sticking the twigs
into the ground, here, there and everywhere.

He must be marking the places where he's going to
plant, thought Jimmy. But before a week was out, the
twigs that at first had wilted and lost their leaves stiffened into life again and put forth new shoots. A

green hand? When Clem stuck a spade into the ground at the end of a day, Jimmy half-expected to see it sprouting leaves by morning. There was nothing Clem couldn't do with a plant. In any weather he'd put down a seed. In any weather he'd take up a seedling. 'It'll be all right if you handle it lightly,' he'd say smiling, planting seeds gaily, with rain falling so heavily on the wet clay that it splashed back into his face and spattered it all over. And when the sun did shine, as often as not he'd be down on his knees with his box of seedlings, pricking them out.

'Won't they die in the sun?' asked Jimmy.

'Why would they die?' cried Clem. 'Like all living things, they only ask to be handled gently.'

To see Clem handle a young plant, you'd think it was some small animal that he held in his hands. Even the seeds got their full share of his love and care, every single one, no matter how many to a packet. Once he nearly made Jimmy scratch up a whole cement floor in the potting shed where he'd let one seed fall.

'We can't leave it there with no food and no drink and no light and no covering,' he cried, as he lit a match to help in the search.

Jimmy felt a bit put upon. 'What about all the packets of seeds that are up there on the shelf?' he protested. 'The last fellow forgot to sow them until it was too late!'

'But it's never too late!' cried Clem. 'Where are they?' And the next minute he had rummaged out the old seeds with their discoloured paper-packets and their faded flower prints. 'Everything should get its chance,' he cried, and he gathered up every flower pot in sight and, filling them with the finest of sieved clay, he poked a seed into each one. 'If there's life in those seeds, they'll take flight before the end of the week!' he told Jimmy. And in less than a week, over each pot there hovered two frail green wings. Yet, for all the energy he spent on plants and chores, Clem still had energy to spare.

'How is the fishing around here?' he asked one evening, a few weeks after his arrival. 'I'd like to take the children fishing. Wouldn't you like to go fishing, Pearl?' he asked, turning to her. She was a good little thing, and she never gave any trouble. All the minding she got was following Clem around the place. Now and again he'd tell her to get up off a cold stone, or to mind would a wasp sting her. There was one thing he was very particular about though, and that was that she should not take off the little woolly coat she always wore.

'Pearly hot!' Pearl would say. No matter! He made her keep the coat on. It was, however, very hot indeed that afternoon in May, and when Clem bent down to dibble in a few colchicums for the autumn, Pearl stamped her foot.

'Pearly hot,' she said, defiantly, and off she took the yellow woolly coat and down she threw it on the ground. Jimmy bent down to pick it up. When he looked up, he was astonished to see Clem's eyes filled with tears. 'I hate anyone to see it,' said Clem. 'I can't bear to look at it myself! But I knew it couldn't be covered forever!'

On the inner, softer side of Pearl's arm was a long, sickle-shaped scar. It was healed. It wasn't really very noticeable. Many a child had a scab twice as big on its knee, or on its elbow, or even its nose! But all the same, Pearl's scar made Jimmy shudder. Perhaps because it was on the soft underflesh, perhaps because of the look it had brought to Clem's eyes, this scar of Pearl's seemed to have a terrible importance.

'Was it an accident, Clem?'

'No,' said Clem shortly.

Could Clem . . . ? But no, no! She was his seedling, his fledgling, his little plant that, if he could, he would cup between his hands, and breathe upon, press close and hold against himself forever. As it was, he put his arms around her. 'Wouldn't you like to catch a little fish, Pearl?' he was asking her. 'I'll get a sally wand for you, and I'll peel it white! You'll catch a great big salmon maybe!'

His own ambition was more humble. He turned abruptly to Jimmy. 'I suppose there's plenty of pike?' he asked. 'Can we get a frog, do you think? Frogs are the only bait for pike. Get hold of a good frog, Jimmy, and we'll meet you down at Cletty Bridge in ten minutes.'

To get a frog on a May evening in Meath! On a wet day, yes – the roads were plastered with them, sprawled out where cars had gone over them. But this evening Clem and the children must have been a full hour down by Cletty pool before Jimmy came running to them, his hand over his pocket.

The children were all calling to each other and laughing, and Clem was shouting excitedly, but it was Pearl's small voice that caught the ear, babbling as joyously to Clem as the pebbles to the stream. There was joy and excitement in the air, and joy welled up in Jimmy's heart, too, as he scrambled over the wall and tumbled happily down the bank, filling the air with the bittersweet smell of elder leaves as he caught at a branch to save himself from falling.

'Good man! You've got the bait!' cried Clem, his expert eye picking out the bulge in Jimmy's pocket. He was helping Pearl to cast her line. It was a peeled willow wand and dangling from it was a big black hairpin bent into a hook. As Jimmy took the frog out of his pocket, however, Clem reached for his own rod which, to have out of harm's way, he had placed crosswise in the cleft of an elder bush that hung over the stream. As he took it down, the taut gut slashed through tender young leaves and, once again, their bitter scent was let out upon the air.

'Here, Jimmy! Here's the hook!' he cried. 'Put on the frog!' Taking a tobacco tin out of his pocket, Clem selected a hook and, fingering it gently free of the other hooks and flies, he laid it in Jimmy's palm. Then he began to unwind his reel. For a few minutes the sound of the winding reel asserted itself over all the other sounds in the glade, until gradually it was absorbed into the general pattern of sound.

Suddenly there was another sound; a horrible sound. It was a screech. And it split the air. It turned every other sound into silence. It was the frog. There was nothing human in that screech, but every human ear in that green place knew what the screech held – it held pain – and pain as humans know it.

'What did you do to him?' yelled Clem, and his face went black with rage. Throwing down the line, he caught hold of the screeching frog. Quick as thought, he pulled out the hook that had only gone a small way into the bulging belly, but had brought out a bubble of its bile-like blood. Then, throwing down the hook and stamping on it, he held the little slimy creature between his two hands.

'You are all right now,' he told it, looking into its bulbous eyes, as if he'd force it to cast out its fear. Then he turned to Jimmy again.' You didn't know any better,' he said sadly. 'You're only a child yourself. But let this be a lesson to you. Never in your life hurt or harm a defenceless thing! Or if you do, then don't let me see you do it! Because I could not stand it. I could not stand it,' he repeated, less gently. 'I never did a cruel thing in my life. I couldn't do one if I tried and – by God's blood – I could not see one done either! I only saw a cruel deed done in my presence once.' Then he lowered his voice so only Jimmy could hear, 'and once was enough! I couldn't stand it!' he cried. 'I couldn't stand it.' And he closed his eyes and pressed his hands over them as if he saw it all again.

When he took down his hands after a minute, and opened his eyes again, he had a dazed look. It was as if he was astonished to find himself there, where he was, on the sunlit bank. More than that – he looked amazed that the sun could shine, amazed that the birds could sing.

'Are you feeling all right?' asked Jimmy.

Clem looked at him dazedly. Then it was as if he took a plunge back into the happiness around him.

'Here, give me a hook!' he cried, rooting around in the box. 'This is the way it's done!' Deftly tucking up the legs of the frog so it fitted snugly into one hand, he nicked it's back with the point of the barb, and then swiftly he passed the hook under the skin and brought it out again as if it were a needle and thread and he had just taken a long, leisurely stitch. 'There! You see! It didn't feel a thing,' he said, and hastily fixing the hook to the end of the line he reeled out a few yards of it and let the frog hang down.

Delightedly he gazed at it for a minute, as it moved its legs rhythmically outward and inward in a swimming motion. 'Wait till we let him into the water!' he cried then, and he ran to the edge of the pool, scattering the children to either side and throwing the line out over the pool. Suspended in the air the frog hung down, as still as the lead on the end of a plumb line, its image given back by the clear water that gave back also the blue sky and the white clouds as if they were under, not over, the pebbles and stones. Then Clem began to unwind the reel, and the frog in the air and the frog in the pool began to draw close to each other, till the real frog hit the water with a smack. Once there, its legs began to work again.

'Swim away, son,' said Clem indulgently, and he unwound more of the line.

'You'd think it was taking swimming lessons, wouldn't you?' he said, watching it amiably.

'But won't the pike eat him?' said Jimmy. 'Isn't that worse than getting the hook stuck in him?'

Clem turned around. 'Nonsense!' he cried. 'Death and pain are two different things. Learn to distinguish, boy!' And he called to Pearl. 'Would you like to hold the line for a while, Pearl?'

But Pearl was not looking at the frog. Something behind them had caught her attention.

'Who are those men, Daddy?' she asked, as two big men in dustcoats, who had been watching the scene for some time from the causeway, began to get over the wall and slide down the bank towards them.

Clem looked back. 'Here, Jimmy,' he said. That was all and he handed him the line.

'You know why we're here?' asked one of the detectives. Clem simply answered their question with a question of his own. 'What about the children?' he asked.

Never would Jimmy have thought that detectives could be so gentle-like and kind. 'The children will be well treated, Clem,' said one. The other addressed Jimmy. 'Stay here with them, you Jimmy, and keep them amused. We've got a woman in the car up on the drive, and she'll come down to you in a minute and see what's to be done.' They turned to Clem. 'We'll have to ask you to come with us, I'm afraid.'

Clem nodded briefly. Then he turned to Jimmy. 'Here, give me the line again for a minute,' he said, and as Pearl had snuggled close to him, her two arms around one leg as if it was a pillar, he freed her grasp and put the rod into her hand.

'You can have the first turn, Pearly,' he said. 'Then Moll. Then the others. After that it will be turn and turn about for you all!' His voice was authoritative, even stern. Then he nodded to the men, and finding it slippery to walk in the dirty tennis shoes, he caught at some of the elder branches, and by their help scrambled up the bank alongside the men.

One Evening

While they were talking Larry leaned his bike against the sooty sycamore tree in the street outside her door. Daylight was leaving the sky. Soon he'd have to go home. He had reached out to grasp the handlebars when the street lamps went on. Startled, he looked up as around them pale light fell like rain. But they, under the dome of leaves, were sheltered from its downpour. A new magic came into their encounter. It was harder than ever to part from her. Overhead, the dusty, toughened leaves of summer appeared thin and silky, as in springtime. If only it was spring and he need not be afraid that they'd be separated when the long school holiday came to an end.

To be nearer to her, he bent forward and rested his elbow on the saddle of the bike, but the springs shifted and, if he had not shot out a hand and steadied himself against the tree, he'd have been sent spinning.

Eileen tittered.

Furious, Larry straightened up and adjusted the saddle before placing his elbow on it once more.

'You nearly fell on your face!' she said.

'And you'd find that funny, I take it? I could have been hurt!'

'That's what I meant,' said Eileen. 'It's a wonder to me you weren't killed years ago on that old bike.'

Mollified by this admission of having known him for years – if only by sight – he gave the frame a rattle. 'It's only fit for scrap,' he said, but he felt disloyal. Except for it, he'd never have struck up acquaintance with her. A fellow couldn't *walk* up and down a street he didn't live on – several times a day, at that – but on a bike it was different. On a bike he could be going anywhere. 'I won't need it after this summer, anyway,' he said. 'Have you decided what you're going to do next year, Eileen?' He ignored the fact that he'd already asked the same question twenty times.

Eileen tossed her head. 'I won't go to the "Uni",', anyway,' she said.

At the abbreviation he squirmed. His father said only outsiders used it. 'But don't you *want* to?' he asked, amazed.

'My sister didn't go, and Pa says she's earning more than any girl with a degree after her name.'

'There are more important things in life than money!' Larry said hotly.

'Oh, I *know*!' Eileen agreed. 'But she has a fellow, *as well*. She goes out with him every evening. He's crazy about her. When he leaves her at home at night, they stand under this tree for ages – kissing and kissing – I can see them from my window.'

Her sister! What did he care about her sister? It was themselves that interested him. 'It's well for them,' he said impulsively.

'What a disgusting thing to say!' Seemingly, though, she was not too repelled, because, putting out her hand, she stroked the handlebars. 'You'd never sell this old bike, would you?' she asked softly. 'It wouldn't fetch much – it's so battered and rusty.' She laughed. 'I used to hear it rattling down the street and I knew it was you – even before I'd met you. Properly, I mean! I remember how you used to stand up on the pedals when the saddle was too high for you. You've no idea how funny you looked!'

'I only did that when I was getting up speed! You used to look pretty funny yourself on your brother's bike with your leg under the crossbar!'

'Oh, do you remember that?'

She seemed delighted, but he'd meant to annoy her the way she had annoyed him. First, all that stuff about her sister! And now this harking back to when they were kids. Gulping down a mouthful of the warm summer air, he thought of a compliment so daring that he felt it must by its utterance turn all their yesterdays into one long tomorrow.

'A nice sight you'd look now on a man's bike!' he cried. And to him the words were so full of innuendo that a smirk came on his face.

But Eileen drew back as if she were stung, and there was fury in her eyes. He thought she was going to slap him. 'How dare you speak to me like that!' she cried. 'Only I know what's wrong with you I'd never speak another word to you ever again in all my life. But you're just peeved because you have to stay home with your mother this evening – and it Sunday and all!'

It was a mean, mean thing to say, but she had reminded him of the lateness of the hour.

'What time is it?' he cried.

Eileen looked oddly at him. 'It must be queer having your father away all week.'

'What's queer about it? Lots of men are only home at the weekends.'

'It's hard on your mother, though, isn't it? – if they get on well together, and all that.'

'What do you mean, "if they get on well together"? You'd think they were a cat and dog!'

Eileen laughed. 'I know some people and they might as well be! Cats and dogs, I mean.' Then she frowned. 'It's hard on you, too – isn't it? – either way. Being all that close to *her*, I mean.'

He wondered what she was getting at; but he could not delay to find out. He sat up on the saddle of the bike, yet kept one leg still on the ground and one hand pressed against the tree.

'I'll have to push off,' he said dejectedly. Eileen had rested the toe of her small patent-leather shoe on the pedal of the bike, and when he did push forward her foot slipped. 'Now who nearly fell on her face!' His spirits were restored: the conversation had come neatly round full circle.

'Well, I like that!' cried the girl. 'There's all the difference in the world between falling and being pushed.'

His good humour trebled. Now he had the advantage. 'Well, so long,' he said, and he wheeled out into the centre of the road and faced for home.

There was nothing like a bike! Standing on the pedals, he pressed down hard on one and then the other, making the old crock rock like a boat. By the time he'd reached the street that went down to the canal alongside which he lived, he'd got up such speed that, as a bird on the hover dips a wing, he had only to drop his shoulder and the bike turned into the sloping street. Then, near the end, dipping the other wing, he swept into Wilton Place.

Between the houses on the Place and the canal bank was a private park, triangular in shape and rarely entered. Such residents as held keys had long ceased to go there. In the middle, the trees had been cut and their stumps were overgrown with moss and ground-ivy so that it was like a forgotten cemetery of a minority sect, Moravian or Huguenot, closed to burials; abandoned. Yet, inside the railings, suckers had sprung up and shrubs and bushes had grown from seed, and here too the trees had not been cut or even pollarded, so that their great, spreading branches filtered the light of the street lamps.

Larry saw at once that there was no light in his own house, or at least not in the front. Moreover, there was something about the dark façade that somehow suggested total darkness.

It was odd. Instead of flinging the bike against the railings and running in, he took a wide sweep out into the roadway to see if any light reflected from the tin roof of the coal shed at the back. Craning his neck as he circled outwards, he nearly bashed head first into a car that was parked with its lights out on the other side of the street. He saved himself just in time, and was startled to discover that it was his father's car. But, if his father was not gone, why was the house in darkness? And why was the car on the other side of the road when there was plenty of space for it outside the door?

There was a figure at the wheel, sitting silent. His father!

Larry's first thought was that his father was dead, but as he jumped off the bike and let it clatter to the ground the headlights were abruptly switched on, almost blinding him.

'Oh, Father! What's up?' he cried. 'Why haven't you gone?'

Overcome by fear, he caught at the door handle, and tried to drag the door open. Immediately, his father's hand shot out and pulled it shut again with a slam.

'Don't mind about me. Go in to your mother,' his father said.

'But the house is all dark, Father. Where is she?'

His father said nothing for a minute. Then he slumped down on the seat. 'I think I killed her,' he said in a quiet, a soft tone. 'You'd better go in.'

'Father!' He could not tell whether to believe or disbelieve, but he started to whimper. 'Oh, Father, Father!' Once more he tried to get into the car, dragging at the handle which his father still held tightly pulled against him. 'Oh, Father, what will you do?' he cried.

Abruptly, then, his father let go the door, which came open, causing Larry to fall backwards; as if he had shaken off something irritating, his father started the engine.

'Where are you going?' Larry cried, agonised.

'Get into the house,' his father ordered.

'Will you come with me?' Larry asked; but even to himself this seemed unreasonable. 'Just as far as the door,' he pleaded. 'Or let me come with you!'

Through the window his father stared at him. 'Why?' he said dully, and then, as if his foot had slipped off the clutch, the car leaped forward.

For a time, the evening was filled with the sound of the departing car, and then there was nothing but the hum of the wheel spokes spinning round on the fallen bicycle.

When the spokes stopped spinning at last, Larry picked up the bicycle and walked it across the street. Inside the front gate, he propped it against the base of a stone balustrade that led up to the hall door. Here, at one time, a plaster cherub had played a flute, but flute and cherub had long been entombed in ivy.

Normally, Larry would have gone in by a door under the steps, because at that hour it was in the basement he would be most likely to find his mother. But noticing that the drawing-room window was open, he went up the steps. By leaning over the balustrade, he might be able to look a little way into the room.

When he reached the top step, however, he was able to see well into the room, for particles of light from the street lamps fell leaf-like through the trees. When the real leaves swayed, the golden foliage swayed, too, this way and that. It was when one of those golden ovals fell evenly over her face that he saw his mother. Still and silent she was, on the couch under the open window. He was so used to seeing her on her feet – she hardly ever sat down except at meals – that he was profoundly shocked by the sight of her. And why did she not call out? She must have seen him! Then the leaves swayed again, and although he could still make out a white blob in the dark he could no longer distinguish her features.

What could he do? There were no people in the street. If there were, how could he approach them? What would he say? Supposing he were to shout – just for anyone to hear – anyone: the people next door or a passerby? But his mother too might hear him, and no matter what was wrong, she would want him to behave in a seemly manner. At last, because he could think of no other way out of the situation, he pushed open the hall door and went in. Taking a deep breath outside the door of the drawing room, he edged around it.

A large splash of light had fallen once again on his mother's face, and he saw that her eyes were open.

'Son!'

'Oh, Mother! Mother!' he cried, his voice torrential

with love. 'Oh, Mother, Mother!' Rushing into the room, he threw himself on her, sobbing with relief.

But, bracing herself against the weight of him, she sat bolt upright. 'What is the matter with you?' she asked angrily.

'Nothing, nothing.' He didn't care that she was cross as long as she was all right. He caught up her hands and began to kiss them. She pulled her hands away.

'What is the meaning of this?' she demanded. 'What is wrong with you? I knew there was something the matter the minute I saw you on the steps. Why were you creeping up like that? And why didn't you speak?'

'Oh, Mother, you don't understand — Father told me —' But he stopped, frightened again.

'Oh?' she said queerly. 'Oh!' And she lay back on the couch. 'So you met him?'

But, surely, sitting there at the open window in the dark, she must have seen them? He moved back from her. 'I'll put on the light,' he said, trying to be matter of fact.

She reached out and caught his hand. 'Not yet,' she said, and there was a pleading note in her voice. 'It's beautiful here with the light coming through the trees. I've been sitting here' — she paused — 'some time,' she finished lamely.

In the dark, he raised his eyebrows. It was not exactly that he thought she was lying, but that he suddenly felt the truth might be more complex than he knew. Then she gave his hand a playful slap.

'I wonder why you were whispering?'

Annoyed, he pulled back.

'I expect you're hungry,' she said when he made no answer. She sighed. 'I suppose I'd better start getting the meal.' But she did not stir.

'I'll lay the table,' he said quickly.

She still made no effort to rise. Instead, she beckoned him back, although he would not have seen that she did were it not for a splash of light that fell on her arm.

'I've never talked much to you about your father, have I?' she said, and he guessed that she was trying to be casual. 'You've never been interested,' she added more coldly, having seen perhaps that he'd stiffened. 'A girl would have been,' she flashed, 'but not a boy! Ah, well. That's another story. Nevertheless, there are certain things you ought to know, things that in later years you will *want* to know: will in fact resent *not* knowing!' Feeling perhaps that this onslaught had subdued him, she settled back into the cushions. 'It was in a room like this,' she said, 'with the street lights coming through the trees like this, that your father first told me he loved me.' Some prudery made her interrupt her story. 'We weren't alone, of course. My mother *and* my sisters were in the next room.' She paused. 'The door was ajar – *always*.' Having eased some scruple, she rushed on. 'I was playing the piano, and your father came and leaned over me.' But the emotion of that dead moment was dead, too. 'I remember the tune exactly!' she cried. 'Every note of it. Although, as you know, I haven't laid a finger on the piano for years.' Her voice changed. 'You *didn't* notice that? You never thought that odd? And yet I used to play with great taste, if not indeed with distinction! Even after you were born.' To his astonishment, there was now a note of admonition in her voice. 'Surely you must remember my playing to you when you were little?' she demanded. 'We had a game. I was a cat and you were a mouse. And as you ran your little fingers up the keyboard I ran mine after you, only you were on the treble and I was on the bass, and you didn't know the difference – you thought the cat's paws made more noise because he was bigger and stronger. You used to beg me to let you be the cat. Do you mean to say you don't remember?' She slid her feet off the couch. 'Let me show you. It will all come back, I feel sure.'

In utter consternation he stared at her. Not for years had the piano been opened. Not since he used to pound on it with clenched fists when she was out of earshot, pretending it was the sound of cannon. He could hardly believe his eyes when she started taking down the silver frames, the vases of dried honesty, and the Venetian glass bluebirds that had stood for a decade undisturbed on the piano top. It was a shock to see how roughly she handled them. And, when she began to pull off the heavy, handmade runner that covered the instrument all over like an altar cloth, he shrank into himself at the thought of the queer, light-coloured wood of the casing being exposed with its birdy-eyed graining and its curlicues. Pianos weren't made of that kind of wood any more.

And so, before a note was struck, he braced himself for the unpleasant sounds that would come from the damp and stuck-together keys. The bass would be no louder than the treble: the cat no better than the mouse.

But things were worse than he'd feared; when his mother ran her hand up and down the notes neither bass nor treble was discernible under the knocking sound of the wooden hammers from which the moth-eaten felting had worn away. Not noticing that any-thing was wrong, however, his mother began playing with both hands, without music, throwing her head back, her body swaying in time to the notes.

'Well, son?'

Hoarsely, he spoke over the din. 'I thought we were going to have our supper.'

Throwing her head back still further, so that she could look at him where he stood behind her, she said archly. 'Time enough. You can't be all that hungry. I want to play something special for you. It's a tune your father used to beg for whenever I lifted the piano lid.' She stopped playing. 'I hope I'll be able to get the opening bar,' she said, dropping her hands into her lap. He felt she did this only for effect.

'I forgot to tell you,' he began desperately, 'that I have to go out tonight.'

She had lifted her hands again and they were poised over the keys, but at his words she let them fall with a thump on to the keys. 'It's Sunday night!'

'I know,' he said weakly. 'I'm sorry.' Then he had

a cunning thought. 'There's no special reason for me staying, is there?' he asked. If, like his father, she too was trying in some crooked way to tell him something . . . well, then, let her tell it straight out. Or else let her keep it. One thing they had both told him without knowing – that they had failed each other. 'You don't really want me for anything special, do you?' he repeated, risking his question in pity for her as he stood in the doorway looking back.

She made no answer except to strike a chord and start to play the tune again loudly. That was the way his father let out the clutch and drove into the night.

'I won't stay out late,' he said, but either she didn't hear him or she scorned this sop. Turning, he ran down the hall in dread that she would follow him. But it seemed that it was only with the tune she tried to follow him, thumping harder on the keys. And even in this purpose she was defeated, for the thick walls, the lath-and-plaster ceiling, and the heavy wooden floorboards absorbed the music. And after he left the house, the only sound that came out into the evening air was the knocking of the clappers and the thump of her foot on the pedals.

Grabbing up the bike, Larry threw his leg across the bar. A last qualm came over him at the thought that his father would blame him for leaving her alone, but his father's stature had been diminished. A man had to be a man. Love could not be kept for ever in the third person, past tense.

A Pure Accident

'Put it out of your mind so, for good and all, will you!' said the Canon. 'You know *my* mind in the matter. It's not a cinema or a public-house we're dealing with: it's the house of God.' The old man prised himself out of his armchair. 'I'll have no hailstorms of light raining down on the heads of *my* people. We have lights enough.'

It was dismissal. The three men sitting around the fire seemed to have no choice but get to their feet and move towards the door after their pastor, but one of them hung back.

'We were only thinking this time of one light in the porch, Canon,' Murty Kane said, ' – or in the chapel yard?'

'No matter,' said the Canon. 'It would still mean rewiring the whole place – and after that there'd be no stopping you: you'd soon have it lit up like the Aurora Borealis.' He himself laughed good-humouredly at this sally, but when the others did not, he looked more closely at them. 'Hold on a minute. Did I ever tell you what I saw when I was in Rome?' he said jovially. 'It was when I was over for the Papal Jubilee – you won't believe it – a sanctuary lamp wired up for electric light! Can you beat that! It's dead against the rubrics.' He leant forward confidentially. 'We had a joke among ourselves – the Irish contingent – we used to laugh our heads off. You know the old proverb "the nearer the church the farther from God"? Well, we used to say "the nearer to Rome the farther from God".'

Here Andy Devine did laugh faint-heartedly, but neither of the others did.

'There was one other point, Canon,' Murty Kane said stoutly. 'If you'd consider the rewiring, we could keep down the number of lights, but we'd be able to have other amenities – like heat.'

'Only a few radiators, Canon,' Andy interjected nervously. 'One in the sacristy, maybe, where the clergy have to robe, another up near the altar, maybe, to keep the altar-linen from getting mildewed, and another . . .'

But at a look from the Canon his voice tailed off.

'Oh, so you *have* something new to bleat about!' the Canon said. 'Well, come back so; come back, by all means.' He closed the door which he had been holding open. He made a feint of squeezing himself down into the tight tub of the chair again, but before doing so he cocked an eye at them. 'I suppose, of course, that you're acquainted with what happened up in Dublin when fellows like you started putting heaters and radiators into the fine old Georgian buildings – those priceless treasures of the nation . . . Well, in case you didn't, let me tell you. They fell down: that's what! Dry rot, that's what! Incubators they made out of them! – and millions of eggs – larvae they're called – hatched out overnight. The damage – in Mountjoy Square alone – ran into millions, to say nothing of the danger to life. A nice set of eejits you'd look if that happened here! You'd never know but the roof might be brought down on top of the people and kill them all.' He let go the chair and stalked over to the door and held it open again. 'Will you never get any sense?' he asked querulously.

In the doorway, however, he seemed unwilling to let them go without a more genial note.

'I don't suppose you men are in the habit of making a visit to the Blessed Sacrament on your way home, but if you should happen to take the notion tonight, just say a few prayers as you stroll past. Don't attempt to go into that chapel.' Surprised, the men who had been looking down at their feet, looked up. 'I've planted Father Patton down there,' said the old man proudly, and he lowered his voice. 'This time I'm determined to catch that thief.'

It was a hard name for a petty pilferer. The men stirred uneasily and looked down at their feet again. Despite the small number of coins ever put into it, the poor box was periodically rifled.

' . . . It's a matter of principle!' said the Canon. 'I've sent Father Patton down there to hide in the porch to see if he can catch the thief red-handed.'

'It's some child, I suppose,' said Andy, feeling that some sort of apology was called for from the laity.

E

'A nice kind of child!' the Canon snapped. 'My only fear is that Father Patton will jump out on the wrong woman.'

But here the men looked up in surprise.

'How do you know it's a woman, Canon?' said Alphonsus Carr.

The Canon gave him a scathing look. 'Is there ever anyone else in the chapel at night only old women? Bundled up in corners, mumbling and jumbling, and thumping their craws! *Mea culpa, mea culpa!* Titillating themselves with piosity – that's all – not a jot of real religion in the lot of them. They ought to be at home looking after their families. But oh no! They must have their nightly jaunt. I often say they couldn't be kept away if it was Satan himself was sitting inside in the Tabernacle, instead of the Son of God!'

But the men weren't listening. Who was it? It could only be someone known to them – well known – a neighbour, a customer – perhaps a relative? They were all so tense suddenly that Alphonsus laughed nervously and he nudged Andy.

'It must be your sister Annie, Andy,' he said. You could set your clock by Annie's step going down to the chapel every night at exactly the same time.

'*That's* who it is!' said Andy, glad to laugh too, because the whole notion of the trap scared him.

'I'd ask you to take this matter seriously, men,' said the Canon coldly. In particular he turned to Andy. 'I certainly hope your sister won't go down there tonight. She could upset the apple-cart altogether.'

Then, as an after-thought, he laid his hand on Andy's arm. 'I'd like you to know it wasn't of her I was thinking when I criticised the other women of the parish. Your sister Annie has no claims on her – a widow woman can do what she likes. How is she, by the way?'

'She's well, thank you, Canon,' said Andy, but his face flushed. He wished his sister's name had not come up. He did not look directly at the Canon, nor at his friends, feeling that his position was never properly understood with regard to Annie.

It was true that Annie had reared him – and his younger brothers – when their mother died, and that when they were old enough to look after themselves she took herself off to America, out of their way. When she came back to Ireland it was by choice she lived alone. He, and his family, had been willing enough to have her live with them, but she was dead set on being independent: she'd made a bit of money over there.

'Ah, she's all right as long as she has the little bit of cash,' said the Canon. 'I hope she doesn't squander it on votive lamps and the like. That money doesn't go into *my* pocket, you know! Tell her that!'

'Oh, she's sensible enough, Canon: no need to worry about her,' said Andy, telling himself his words were true.

The Canon nodded. 'All the same, I hope she won't put a spoke in Father Patton's wheel tonight. Poor Patton: I'm afraid he's no man for this job. He'll botch it! If he finds any candles lighting I hope he'll have the sense to quench them, or else all he'll catch will be a cold in the head.'

When the men *did* laugh at that, the Canon was better satisfied to let them go. His voice became more amiable. 'Poor Patton!' he repeated. 'You'd feel sorry for him if you'd seen him going out tonight – he was in a blue funk!'

All of them for a moment thought about Father Patton: a large man of middle years, whose bulk made him look aggressive, but who in fact was timid enough, and whose aspect in the presence of the Canon was abject.

'It's hard to see what sends the likes of him into the Church at all,' sighed the Canon. 'They do their best, I grant you, but they don't have the right motive at the start. Pushed from behind – that's what they are! Oh, the mothers of Ireland – they have a lot to answer for! When I was in Maynooth I used to see them on visiting day walking around the grounds with their poor weedy, pimply-faced sons, and they wrapping their own mufflers around the poor fellows' necks, and giving them their own gloves to put on their hands, instead of letting them stiffen into men of their own making. Ah, the right kind of mother is a rare creature. My own mother – God be good to her – would as soon have seen me a bank manager, but when I made my choice she put all her weight behind me. No wonder I have contempt for poor slobs like Father Patton.' Then his face grew stern again. 'I hope he won't scruple putting out the candles. That chapel is a regular Crystal Palace at times, with candles and colza lamps. What do you think? Will he have the wit to quench them?'

Was he joking? A Crystal Palace! The men stared at each other.

But the Canon had opened the door and was showing them into the hallway. 'We can only hope for the best,' he said affably. 'Goodnight, men.'

It was not customary for the Canon to accompany them to the hall-door, but as they slammed it after them, a light over the steps was switched on from within. However, as soon as they got to the bottom step, this light went out abruptly. And, accustomed as they were to being thus plunged into darkness, there was always a slight shock. On this particular night Andy stumbled over the iron footscraper.

'The sky seems to have clouded over since we went in,' he said, to cover his confusion.

Alphonsus looked up. 'I thought the forecast gave frost,' he said. 'It may come later, of course.'

The Canon's driveway was short but dark and the men had to pick their way carefully on the thick gravel that rolled under their feet like shingle. Away to the left, there was a glow in the sky, like the after-glow of sunset, but it was in fact a reflection of the lights of the town.

'You'd think it was the city of Dublin,' said Murty sourly.

It was a sore point with all three men that the

Market Square was so well lighted. In the evenings it became the centre of all activity; all conviviality. Shops like their own in the back streets could put up their shutters once darkness fell for all the business they'd do. On fine evenings people stood about in the Square reading the paper by the light of the shop windows as if by daylight. The big shops had to have spikes set into the window-sills to prevent them being used as public benches!

'Does it pay them, I wonder, to burn all those lights?' said Andy, coughing gently as he looked again at the glow in the sky.

'They may have no option,' said Alphonsus. 'It's probably a condition laid down by the insurance company.' His friends understood, of course, that he was speaking especially of the public-houses.

'I suppose you're right, Alphonsus,' said Andy. 'God knows they need light with the footless crowd that's in there at night. They spend most of the time stumbling in and out to the lavatory in the yard.'

But now they had reached the end of the Canon's drive, and, feeling their way, they found the wicket-gate, and went out one by one on to the road.

'You'd think they could have put a few more lamps on this road, seeing it's the chapel-road,' said Andy.

'Why should they?' Alphonsus dissented. 'The chapel is the concern of the Canon. It's up to him to see that the area around it is lighted. I don't think it would be too much to expect him to put one light over the gate!'

But at that Murty gave a short laugh.

'Are you joking?' he said. 'When he can't be got to light the inside, he's hardly going to illuminate the outside! After tonight we may as well throw in our hand. We'll never best him now. It's my opinion that man wouldn't part with a penny if it was to save his soul – in a manner of speaking,' he added awkwardly, when the others laughed.

But whether or not the joke was intentional, his companions – not being responsible for the irreverence – felt free to go on laughing. Then Murty sobered up.

'Has he much money, would you say?' he asked. 'The Canon, I mean?'

Alphonsus shrugged his shoulders. 'Who knows!'

'Where *does* a priest's money go anyway when he dies?' Murty asked after a minute or two. 'Can he leave it to anyone he wants – like an ordinary person – or does he have to leave it to the Church? Come to think of it, I never saw a priest's will in the paper! But I suppose it's seldom a priest has anything to leave behind!'

'Oh, I wouldn't be too sure of that,' Alphonsus said. 'A will doesn't have to be published in the papers unless there is a specific bequest to charity, and–'

But here Andy interrupted him. 'Ah sure. God help them,' he murmured, 'who'd expect them to give to charity: aren't their whole lives devoted to the sick and the suffering. . . .'

Alphonsus nodded. ' . . . and the dying,' he said. 'And the bereaved! It'd only be fair that they'd be free after their death to leave any few pounds they might have to a niece or a nephew. After all, their families were deprived of them as wage-earners, and I'm told that in some cases their families have to go on contributing to their support even after they're ordained – holidays and the like – '

'Ah, but that latter is not so common, I'd say,' said Andy, striking a nice balance between censuring and condoning. 'Most of them make out all right; they don't have too bad a time, all things considered.'

This was the part of the evening he enjoyed best when, after a scrap with the Canon, they strolled home, their humour restored by their own affability.

They had now passed the last lamp-post between the parochial house and the chapel, and when they had gone beyond its hooded circle of light, ahead of them, blacker than night, loomed the chapel and its sepulchral yard. Instinctively the men came to a stand at the gateway and looked inward. Ordinarily, through the narrow windows, there would be a soft gleam of candlelight, but tonight it seemed as black as pitch. It was not even certain whether the door of the big front porch was open or shut.

'Father Patton must be still in there,' said Andy, and he shuddered. 'I wouldn't like his job.' He peered in the gate. 'He couldn't have put out the sanctuary lamp, could he?' he said then, in a shocked voice.

'What harm if he did: it's not dogma,' said Alphonsus impatiently. 'It's only a pious custom.' He too, was straining his eyes into the dark. 'It *is* lighting anyway,' he said, as in the deep recesses of the cavern he could just make out the imprisoned flame burning in its pool of oil, but dispensing no rays.

Murty turned and peered across the road.

'Look!' he said. 'There's his car!' Pulled in under the trees on the opposite side of the road was the curate's old car.

'He didn't catch anyone yet!' said Andy, vaguely relieved. 'Maybe his car was seen.'

'Just as well!' said Murty. 'What loss is a few coins compared to someone's character?'

Openly relieved, the three men were starting to walk forward again when they heard bright ringing steps coming towards them in the dark.

There was no mistaking those footsteps.

'It's Annie,' Andy said, and he couldn't keep dismay out of his voice.

'Do you think we ought to warn her?' Murty said, and his voice, too, was oddly urgent.

'No, no. Why would we?' said Andy, pulling himself together. He was oddly nettled by Murty's concern. Anyway, his sister was stepping out so briskly she was almost abreast of them.

'Goodnight all,' she said, in her clear voice that always surprised by its youthful note. The next minute she had passed them and turned in the chapel gateway. They heard her heels tap-tapping on the hard impacted gravel.

'Isn't she an active woman for her years?' said Alphonsus.

'She was always the same,' said Andy. He was pleased at the compliment to her. 'That's what I remember most about her when she was young. I'd lie in bed at night listening to her feet on the flagstones down under me, until the sound would put me to sleep – like music. And I missed it when she went away to America.' He laughed softly. 'When she came back, though – the time she was staying with us before she got her own little house – it used to drive us all mad then to hear her tapping about below until all hours. One night I asked her to take off her shoes, but the next day I had to tell her to keep them on, because in her stocking-feet she hammered around even harder!'

'Oh, she's a strong woman: there's no doubt of that!' said Murty. 'And let me tell–' But here he stopped, as, incredibly, the night was rent with a scream. 'What was that?'

Shocked, they all came to a stand. It was the scream of a young woman. And yet it must have been Annie.

'It couldn't be Annie!' said Alphonsus, speaking for them all, but they started to run back to the chapel gate, when suddenly Father Patton's voice was heard. They stopped.

'Ah, she got a fright, that's all,' said Andy, reassured.

They listened. 'In the name of God, what's the

matter with you, woman?' the curate cried. 'Get up out of that!'

'Oh, Father, I'm sorry.' It *was* Annie's voice. It was a relief to hear it so normal. 'I didn't see you standing there in the dark, Father, and then when I brushed against you and you moved, I didn't know who it was' – but here her voice wavered and the listeners lost something. The next minute there was another small scream but again Annie's voice came to them clear and strong. 'Don't! Don't, Father,' she cried. 'I'll get up by myself – if I'm able.'

But now Father Patton was shouting. 'If you're able! And why wouldn't you be able?'

'Oh Father, I think I'm hurt,' Annie said, and she gave a moan.

Murty started. 'Did you hear that?'

'Wait, Murty,' said Andy, and he put up his hand. 'We don't want to embarrass Father Patton.'

They listened.

'Of course you're hurt,' said the priest. 'Wouldn't it hurt an ox to come down on his backside the way you did – it isn't going to do you any good to lie there on the ground. Get up out of that – I've got the car outside and I'll run you home.' He must have tried to lift her again because Annie gave another scream, or a sort of scream. The three men waited no longer.

'We're here, Annie,' Murty called. 'You'll be all right.'

Andy addressed himself to the curate. 'She'll be all right, Father – she only got a fright. You'll see. . . .'

The clouds had thinned out and the faint light in the sky made it possible for them all to see each other. Annie lay on the ground, the curate bending over her.

'Such a night I've had,' said the curate, straightening up. 'This is the last straw.' He stepped back and looked in the direction of the parochial house. 'That scream must have been heard all over the town!' he said. Then he turned back. 'What kind of a woman is she to scream like that? And what's the matter with her that she won't get up?' He pushed Andy forward. 'Make her get up!'

But Annie caught Andy's hand. 'I'm sorry, Andy,' she said. 'I couldn't help it. I think I hurt myself – my side is very sore.'

Only the last word caught the priest's ear.

'Sore? Hurt?' he shouted. 'What else did she expect coming down on her arse like that? We've got to get her out of here. If this caper gets to the ears of the Canon there's no telling the harm it could do me! I'll tell you what – I'll bring the car in here. Let you three get her on her feet.'

'Wait a minute, Father!' Murty called after him. 'Maybe we ought to get a doctor to have a look at her before we try to move her.'

'Is it out to make a show of me altogether you are, Murty Kane?' the priest cried. 'It's bad enough that some other old woman may come along any minute and start poking her nose into our business. Here – I won't wait to get the car. Give me a hand with her and we'll carry her out if she won't co-operate.'

The path was narrow, and to lift her Andy and Murty had to step on to the grass verge. Under their feet the grass was crisp and brittle. Looking up, Andy saw that a high wind had cleared the sky and now it was dizzy with stars. The forecast was right. There was frost after all.

'Be patient, Annie, be patient. We're doing our best,' he said, embarrassed by the way she kept moaning.

At the gate, Father Patton let go his hold to run across the road and bring over the car. As it swept around in a circle, the headlights for a moment ripened the frosty grass to a golden stubble. Then Father Patton shut off the lights again and got out.

'All together, men!' he said, and they bundled the woman into the back seat.

When they arrived at Annie's little house, they had more difficulty getting her out than they had getting her in, but they managed it. Where was the key of the house, though?

'It's in her bag I suppose,' said Andy, seeing with surprise that through thick and thin Annie had held tight to her bag. But now the shabby black bag gaped open.

Father Patton shook it.

'The key must have fallen out; we'll have to bring her to your place, Andy,' he said.

Gathering every dreg of strength left in her, however, Annie cried out in anguish. 'No, no, no! You can't put me into that car again. Is it trying to kill me you are?'

'Don't heed her,' cried Father Patton. 'Catch her up there.'

This time, though, when Annie was in the car again and Andy had squeezed in with her, Murty stepped back.

'You can leave me out of this from now on,' he cried.

Father Patton turned and gave him a look, then he dived into the car. 'Come on,' he said to the others. 'We're in trouble enough as things are.'

A big, heavily moving man, Father Patton usually drove slowly, but tonight as the car careened along, although Alphonsus caught first at the door-handle, and then at the back of the driver's seat, he was rocked violently from side to side, and when, without slowing up, they shot into the lighted Square, he saw that the priest's face was livid and fixed in a stare. Fearfully Alphonsus looked around at the others. On the back seat Andy had put his arm around Annie, hugging her to him like a lover. Brother and sister stared in front of them unseeing; the eyes of one prised open by fear, the other by pain. The next instant the car hurtled down another side-street and all was dark again.

At Andy's gate it stopped, and Father Patton turned around and looked into the back.

'What kind of a heart has she, Andy?' he asked.

'Oh, her heart is all right,' Andy answered. 'As strong as a lion.'

But suddenly, with a convulsive jerk, Annie pulled away from her brother and caught at his arm. 'Andy!'

she cried, 'there's something sticking into me – into my arm!'

Before Andy could say anything the curate's voice rose in fury. 'What's wrong with her now?' he yelled. 'First her arse, and now her arm!'

Alphonsus drew a sharp breath. 'Look here, Father,' he said hotly, 'this is the second time tonight you've used that word.'

'Oh please, Alphonsus, please!' Andy pleaded. 'Father Patton is upset too. We must make allowances.'

But Annie had leaned forward and caught Alphonsus by the hand.

'Could there be something broken inside me, Alphonsus?' she cried, and she pulled his hand down 'Feel!'

Taken by surprise at the strength of her hands, Alphonsus felt his own hand pressed against her thigh, from which, although muffled by clothing, something hard stuck up.

'Christ!' he exclaimed, and dragged his hand free. 'It's the bone!'

'Oh no, no, no!' Annie started to cry.

Everyone else was struck dumb, and the curate, putting his hands up to his head, began to sway back and forth. It was at that moment that the lights of another car behind flashed over them like the beam of a lighthouse.

'A car! Stop it!' cried Annie. 'For God's sake don't let it pass.'

Andy and Alphonsus got out to flag it down, but

the car was pulling up beside them, and out of it jumped Murty Kane, shaking his fist in the air.

'Did you think I was going to stand by and let you add murder to everything else!' he cried, but the doctor who accompanied him and was getting out on the other side cut him short.

'That's enough, Murty,' he said. Taking a torch out of his pocket, the doctor flashed it into the priest's car, and ran his hand over Annie's body. Straightening up he hurriedly started to prepare an injection. 'What kind of fools are you?' he said in an angry voice. 'God alone knows what damage you've done. But after this at least she won't feel any more till we get her to hospital.' He put the syringe back into his pocket. 'You'd better get her there as fast as you can.' As no one moved, he looked sharply at the priest. 'Pull yourself together, Father. You're not out of the wood yet.'

Like a sleep-walker, Father Patton turned on the ignition. Then, as Andy was about to squeeze into the back again the doctor took him by the arm.

'Get into the front, you,' he said. Without a word, Murty and Alphonsus stepped aside and, as when a hearse is about to drive away, they took off their hats. 'There's just one thing!' the doctor called out, dragging open the door again. 'I'll be 'phoning the hospital – where do you want her put – in a public ward or a private?'

The curate's foot was on the clutch. He turned to Andy. 'She has some means, hasn't she?'

'Oh yes – she has a little!' said Andy. 'She was a

thrifty woman.' He looked into the back seat as if for confirmation, but Annie was already unconscious. 'I suppose she deserves the best after all she's been through,' he said.

'She'll get that in either place,' said the doctor curtly, and then ignoring Andy, he spoke to the priest. 'We don't want to cripple her in every way! What do you think will be the outcome of this? Will she get compensation?' As the priest gave no answer the doctor slammed the car-door. 'Settle it among yourselves,' he said impatiently. 'Money may not be the worst of your worries.'

It was three days before Andy saw his sister. Her bed was in the centre of a large room, and when he edged around the door two nurses were cranking up a kind of jack which slanted the bed upwards. Although flat on her back Annie was looking straight at him.

Brother and sister stared at each other.

'How are you, Annie?' said Andy.

It was one of the nurses who answered.

'Oh, we're splendid!' she said brightly, and she looked at Annie. 'Aren't we?'

Annie's eyes were very bright. 'They operated on me, Andy. I have a silver pin in my hip!' she said. She paused. 'I'm told I stood it well. What did they tell you?'

'Oh, they work wonders nowadays,' said Andy quickly. One of the nurses – the younger one – had gone out of the room, and he wished the other one

F

would go too. 'You've a nice room, Annie,' he said.

Annie looked around the room. 'Yes, it's nice,' she said politely.

'Did you see her flowers?' the nurse asked.

Looking, Andy saw that in a vase beside the bed there were several sprays of leafless white lilac, on long woody stems.

'Alphonsus and Murty sent them,' said Annie. 'Fancy lilac at this time of year, Andy!'

There didn't seem to be any perfume from the fronds of forced blooms.

'They have no smell!' said Andy.

Both Annie and the nurse seemed surprised.

'What else could you expect at this time of year?' said the nurse, but bending she looked more critically at the lilac. Then she snatched at a spray and lifted it out of the vase. Shaking off the water, she examined it closely. 'This one can go!' she cried. She snatched out another. 'And this!'

'Oh, Nurse, they're still fresh!' cried Annie.

But the nurse was scrutinising every stem, her practised eye finding the first frail freckle of decay on the lovely lilac petals.

'I hate the smell of rotting flowers,' she said. 'They don't last any time in these overheated rooms.' Breaking the discarded branches in two she threw them into a waste-can. As she did, a faint scent was shaken from them, and for an instant it streamed in the air. She turned to Andy. 'You may stay as long as you like!' she said affably, and she went out.

Left alone, the sister and brother looked at each other again. 'How are you feeling?' Andy asked.

Annie, however, was looking past him towards the door which the nurse had left ajar. 'Why didn't she close it?' she asked. 'There isn't anyone outside, is there?'

'No – who would there be?' said Andy. 'Didn't Alphonsus and Murty *send* flowers?' He spoke as if answering a charge.

'Oh, I didn't expect *them* to come,' said Annie. 'Not so soon anyway. They'll probably come in some time in the car with Father Patton.'

Andy's face brightened. 'Oh, is he coming?' he asked. 'When? Did he send word?'

'No – but don't you know he will,' said Annie. 'I thought he might have come with you today.'

Andy looked down at his feet. 'He had to go to a funeral today. Anyway, he was very upset, Annie.'

'About me?'

'Upset generally.'

There was a short silence. Again Annie glanced at the open door. 'You're *sure* there's no one outside?'

'Ah, who would there be?' said Andy irritably for one of his disposition.

'Well, shut it, will you?' said Annie, and her voice too was short. When the door was shut they both felt better. 'I'd like him to know how sorry I was that I gave him all that trouble, but the pain put everything out of my head. Oh, Andy, wasn't it an unfortunate thing to happen? And in the chapel of all places!'

'Now, now, Annie,' said her brother. 'What difference where it happened!' But as this bit of philosophy didn't seem to help Annie, he plunged in the opposite direction. 'All the more reason to take it well,' he said. 'There must have been a purpose in it. My advice is not to think about it. Make the most of things while you're here. Make a holiday out of it!' he cried, his voice rising.

Annie tried to smile, but as she did so the remaining sprays of lilac caught her eye and she frowned. 'That lilac wasn't in the least withered. She wouldn't have been so quick to throw it out if it was her own, or if she'd paid for it with her own money.' Then, surprisingly, she giggled. 'Of course, it wasn't my money either!' Her face clouded once more. 'Who *is* paying for everything, Andy?' she asked anxiously.

'Now, now,' said Andy soothingly. 'Your job is to get well and not to be worrying about things like that.'

'But who *will* pay it, Andy?' she persisted.

Andy stood up. 'When you talk like this, it's time for me to go,' he said. 'Worry isn't good for you. All you have to do is lie back and let them put you right – and be glad you're well cared for and comfortable.'

'Oh, there's no doubt I'm well minded,' said Annie. 'I'd be having the time of my life if I wasn't worrying about who's going to pay!' It seemed however as if the visit had taxed her strength because she closed her eyes.

'Well then, don't think about it!' said Andy, and

as he thought she seemed sleepy, he got to his feet.
He might as well go.

At the end of a month Annie was let try out her
legs. She was very nervous but the rest in bed had done
her good and she looked well. Along with worrying
about the bill, though, it bothered her that Father
Patton had not called to see her, although Murty and
Alphonsus confirmed what Andy had told her earlier:
the curate was in a bad state. They kept telling her that
her accident had shaken him. Yet, at the end of
another month Annie was still expecting him. Andy
had come to dread the mention of his name.

'You don't understand, Annie,' he said. 'We're all
worried about him. There's a great change in him. He
looks dreadful. Only last night we were saying that
this thing is getting on his nerves.'

'Does he ask for me?' Annie asked.

'Well, the fact is,' said Andy, 'we don't see much of
him. He went away somewhere the day after the
accident – didn't I tell you that? – and you know he
never goes anywhere, but now he's always taking off
on short trips without telling anyone, or saying where
he's going – Murty thinks there must be something
on foot. He thinks it could be down to his brother's
place he goes – he has a brother, a chemist somewhere
in the Midlands. . . . We used to think there was no
love lost between him and the brother, but maybe the
brother is going to put up something towards your
expenses.'

Annie sat up straighter. 'And who'd put up the rest?' she asked eagerly. 'The Canon?'

'Are you raving, Annie?' said Andy. 'Isn't that the whole trouble? The Canon knows nothing about your accident – he knows you're in here, of course – but he doesn't know why . . .' Annie's brightness faded, and Andy saw she really didn't look as well as he'd thought at first. 'One good thing has come out of it all,' he said nervously. 'We're determined to try once more to get a light put in the porch of the chapel. You'll have the satisfaction of knowing that what happened to you won't happen again, anyway.'

Dully Annie looked at him. 'It's not much satisfaction, is it?' she said.

'Oh come now,' said Andy. 'You're getting depressed. Do you think you might rest if I wasn't here?'

'No,' said Annie. She looked at the clock. 'Anyway I have my therapy at four o'clock. They've been taking me down in the lift, but today they're going to see if I can manage the stairs.' She looked around. 'I've got a new stick. Did you see it? The other one belonged to the hospital: this will be my own.' Suddenly her face clouded again. 'Who's going to pay for that' – she cried – 'the stick? This isn't an ordinary stick. It may *look* ordinary but I'm sure it will cost a lot. And the therapy! – what will that cost? It will be extra. On top of everything else!'

Andy said nothing for a minute. Then he had an

idea. 'Maybe all this therapy, as you call it, isn't necessary. When they get people into these places they take advantage of them; you know that.'

'Do you think so?' Annie's face puckered. 'I'm having massage too, did I tell you that? They say my muscles will seize up if I don't – and then I'd be a *real* invalid! Oh Andy, will I ever be able to manage when I do go home?'

'Oh come: we'll face that when we get to it,' said Andy hastily. 'The bill is enough to worry about now.' The last words dropped out accidentally, but it scared him to see how they affected Annie.

'I thought you weren't worried about that at all?' she cried.

'Oh, I'm not really,' said Andy hastily. 'Maybe no one will be called upon to pay,' he added recklessly. 'The Church is very influential, you know.'

Annie brightened again. He was tempted to leave quickly while her spirits were up, but she leant forward eagerly.

'That's what one of the wardsmaids said. . . . She was telling me about a woman who – '

Andy interrupted her. 'I'm surprised at you, Annie,' he said. 'Why do you listen to people like that. . . ? This is not America, you know.' It was her years in America that blinded her to the difference between people, he thought. Annie lay back on the pillows.

'I think a lot about America since I came in here,' she said, and she looked around her. 'This room is a bit like my room in the apartment-house in New York.

I was thinking it was a pity I came home when I did: I'd have made a lot more money by now.'

'You did well enough,' said Andy curtly, 'and there's no use crying over spilt milk.'

But the next week when he came in to visit her, Andy saw at once that Annie was very upset. She was up hobbling round the room, and didn't hear him come through the door until he spoke.

'Oh Andy!' She sort of ran towards him, which was very distressing because of how she lurched and rose, lurched and rose. Like a boat, he thought. He took the stick from her and made her sit down. 'Oh Andy,' she cried, 'they mentioned the bill. They asked me if it was to you they'd send it.'

'To me?'

Andy was speechless. His eyes fastened on the stick. She was right: it wasn't an ordinary one. It had a rubber hand-grip, and at the base it widened out into a flat metal disc that was set in a sort of rubber coaster. He had no idea what a stick like that would cost, but it wouldn't be cheap; that was certain. All the pent-up worry of the past months broke suddenly.

'Annie – you wouldn't consider, would you . . .' He stopped. 'I mean the simplest thing might be to pay the bill yourself. . . .' But at the look of panic that came over her face he patted her on the knee. 'When you come home you could talk it over with Father Patton – you'd only be advancing the money, as it were. . . .'

Annie shook off his hand. 'With what would I pay?' she cried. 'I'd have to sell my American shares, and then what would I have to live on?'

Andy couldn't answer this directly, but he shook his head. 'I never felt happy about those paper investments,' he said.

'Oh Andy!' No wonder the family business had gone downhill. A thought – the very opposite of what she had lately been thinking – about staying in America – came into her mind. She ought never to have gone. She sighed. One or the other. Certainly as a business man Andy was a poor specimen. Then she straightened up as well as she could. 'I'll have to see a solicitor, that's all,' she said.

Andy started. 'And what solicitor do you think you'd get?' he cried. No decent firm would take the case, once the clergy was concerned. 'I'm telling you, the best thing would be to pay it if you could at all. You wouldn't lose by it, Annie. I feel sure of that. You'd get it all back a hundred-fold.'

Annie looked up. It was as if all along there had been a stupid misunderstanding that was suddenly being cleared.

'From whom?'

Her brother seemed surprised that she should ask. 'From the Giver of all things, Annie. Who else?'

'Oh Andy! You gave me such a disappointment.' To her brother's dismay her eyes filled with tears. And he realised that he had never before seen her cry – in all his life, not even when he was a child and she was only a young girl, shouldering the burthen of their orphaned home.

'Oh, you might get some shady solicitor to take it on,' he said quickly, in order to let her down a bit more lightly. 'You wouldn't stoop to that I know,' he added.

But how did he know she wouldn't? He himself was overcome by such misery he put his head in his hands. 'Oh Annie, Annie, is there no way we could get the money and at the same time spare Father Patton?'

His mind was so muddled he hardly knew what he was saying. But like long ago, Annie's mind was crystal clear; and her voice a crystal bell.

'Spare him from what?' she asked. Pushing aside the medicine bottles on the bedside table, she took up a pen. 'I'm going to write and tell him to call. You can give him the letter on your way home, or put it in his letterbox if you like.'

'Oh Father!' Annie cried out in genuine surprise when the next morning, before she was out of bed, the door opened and Father Patton lunged into her room.

In the small room he looked bigger and bulkier than ever. Annie felt that if she were on her feet there wouldn't be a place for the two of them in the one room. She waited nervously for him to speak. As he said nothing, she glanced at the window where a spate of rain rattled the panes.

'What a terrible day to have brought you out, Father,' she said.

But she felt frightened when the curate moved over towards the bed. 'It's not the weather that's bothering me,' Father Patton said. As he came nearer, Annie saw that his hands were trembling. 'How are you?' he asked, but seeing that she was looking at his hands, he stared down at them himself. 'That's nothing,' he said, and he raised his arm to expose the armpit. 'Look at that sweat. It keeps pouring out of me. My suit is destroyed. And my other suit is worse – the one I was wearing that night. I sent it to be cleaned, but they couldn't do anything with it, the armpits were rotted. I'll have to throw it away. . . .'

'You got a shock, Father,' said Annie gently. 'I know that, and I'm sorry.'

The curate looked strangely at her. Disarmed by her gentleness, he relaxed.

'What in the name of God were you doing that night creeping about in the dark?' he said. 'If you'd any sense it's at home in your bed you'd have been – an old woman like you!' But here he drew himself up. 'That's not what I came to say though. I came to make it clear that I have no money to pay your bills!'

'Nobody expects you to pay anything, Father,' said Annie, less gently. 'Nobody expects a priest to have money of his own, but – '

Father Patton had to interrupt her. 'Ah, you're wrong there! You'd be surprised how many have money! Some I know seem to make out all right – holidays in Kilkee, and a decanter always at their elbow – but let me tell you it's not the parish that pays for it – it's their own families. That's where I lose out – with only one brother and him with a grudge against me.' Unable to stay still, he began to pace around waving his hands. Then abruptly he came to stand again at the foot of the bed. 'The day after it happened I went and had a talk with him. Do you think I got any sympathy? None. But I might have known! He was always sour about the money that was spent on me. Only for that he'd have been a doctor instead of only a chemist – and in a small town at that. So you see,' he said, leaning down heavily on the iron bed-rail, 'you're flogging a dead horse!'

Dazed by the spate of words Annie's head began to reel, but she forced herself to concentrate.

'What about the Canon?' she said then, deliberately.

Father Patton let go the rail. 'Is it him?' he cried. 'Your fall must have made you soft in the head. Isn't it his meanness has me the way I am!'

Annie put her hands under her and hoisted herself up in the bed. 'Then what about the Bishop? Couldn't you approach him?'

As if unable to believe he had heard aright, the curate could only glare at her. But Annie didn't flinch, and he was forced to reply.

'It's easy to see how little the laity know about the clergy,' he cried. 'Don't you see that would be playing right into their hands, giving them the chance they've always been looking for. . . .'

Annie put up her hand to her throat. He was suffocating her with words.

' . . . the chance for what?'

He glared again. 'As if you didn't know! I could be clapped back there again,' he said wildly.

'Back where?'

'Oh, you know very well,' said the curate. 'Nobody ever mentions it, but I'm not taken in – it's known to all – John of God's – that's where! Don't pretend you've never heard.'

For the second time Annie felt frightened.

'You're letting this get on your nerves, Father,' she said.

Her words were ill-chosen. 'There, you see!' he cried. 'The same thing on your tongue as on everyone else's. *"It's your nerves, Father. Steady down, Father. Pull yourself together, Father."* ' He had caught the bed-rail again, but now his hands were shaking so much the bed rocked like a cradle.

'Oh Father, Father, *please!*' Annie's face twisted with pain, but it wasn't certain whether it was caused by the shaking of the bed or by the priest's words.

Ignoring her cry and with a wild look on his face the curate went on.

'My only chance is to keep in the Bishop's good books.' Then suddenly another aspect of the situation seemed to strike him. 'It's *your* only chance too,' he cried. 'Don't tell me you're blind to the advantage to you in me getting a parish – or even getting out of this one and getting away to some place where I'd have some sort of life of my own. But one word of this in the ear of the Bishop and all hope of that is gone forever. And let me tell you that it would be the end of your expectations too. Oh yes! don't think my ruination would serve you any good.' But the thought of his own ruin overwhelmed him. 'How would you like to have it on your conscience that you destroyed me?' he cried. He let go the rail, but he could not stop talking. 'If you've once been in John of God's they have it marked up against you for life. It wouldn't make any difference my being as right as rain – like the last time. . . .'

To make sure she was heeding him he gave the bed-rail a rattle. 'There was nothing wrong with me the last time either, only that I was a gom: I didn't realise all the *other* fellows were going through the same thing as me, only *they* were always rushing about on the hurley field, and running up and down in the mud till they stupefied themselves, but I kept trying to work everything out in my head, walking the floorboards at night, all alone, destroying my strength, and getting unfitter and unfitter to make up my mind about anything. A few fellows left that year, but I kept going round in circles till it came to the point where I was told I'd be *put* out! That was when the real trouble began. My mother wouldn't hear of them putting me out. She said it was only nerves. She held that I'd be all right if I got a bit of peace and quiet.'

Here the priest's voice sank so low Annie could hardly hear it, and leaning his two elbows on the rail he hid his face in his big bulky hands. When he looked up again there was no expression at all on his face.

'My mother was right about one thing, God be good to her!' he said. 'There was nothing wrong with me. After a few weeks of sleeping late and walking in the garden I was well enough to go back to the seminary, and they let me go forward for ordination. Not with my own class-men, though! I was put back a year. And that was where I lost my foothold. I fell behind then, and when you do that you never catch up again. I ought to have had a parish long ago. Doesn't everyone know that?'

When he first started talking he had become very wild and distraught, but it seemed that unravelling back to those early days gave him some peace.

'I wouldn't have minded being delayed in getting a parish if I had been sent to a place where the parish priest would be on my side, and put in a good word for me. They can do that, you know! They often get the ear of the Bishop at Confirmation, or at the Priests' Retreat, or better still, in places like Kilkee or Tramore, where they all flock for their holidays. But the man I'm up against wouldn't put in a good word for a saint. And he gave up going on holidays years ago. He wouldn't give it to say he'd spend money on himself in case his curate would expect to have some spent on him. And it's not as if I could hope he'd be called to his reward, because he's the kind will live for ever. I'll never get a parish! Never! I'll always be like a cockroach, crushed under somebody's foot.'

To Annie's consternation tears suddenly brimmed into his eyes and spilled out and ran down his big face, even into his mouth. 'A cockroach!' he sobbed.

Utterly shocked, Annie stretched out her hands to him. 'Please don't, Father!'

But once started, the crying couldn't be stemmed.

'Oh stop, Father, stop, stop, please!' Annie cried to no effect.

Catching at her stick that rested against the bed-table, she tried clumsily to get out of bed and go to him, but the stick fell and the medicine bottles on the table wobbled as her arm knocked against them.

'You'll be heard outside, Father,' she cried. 'The nurses will hear you: they'll come in to see what's the matter.' Indeed, just then she heard the rattle of crockery outside the door. 'Oh quick!' she cried. 'They're bringing round the dinners: they'll walk in on us.' Pulling out a handkerchief she tried to throw it to him, but it fluttered on to the counterpane halfway down the bed. 'You don't want to be seen like this, do you?' she pleaded.

It was too late. The wardsmaid had come in the door. She was a big country girl and she was holding the tray high, so she didn't see the visitor. But Father Patton turned on her.

'Put down that tray and get out of here quick!' he shouted.

The girl's mouth opened and she came to a stand in the doorway. The tray tilted.

'Watch out!' Father Patton shouted. 'You're going to spill that slop!' His swollen eyes travelled over the girl. 'Put it down and get out, like I said!' he cried.

'Stir your stumps!' But as the girl, blushing furiously, stood rooted to the floor, he snatched the tray out of her hands, and planted it down himself on Annie's lap.

'Oh mind! Father, it's scalding hot!' the girl cried, coming to her senses. The room was filling with a hot smell of boiled fowl and onion.

'It smells good I must admit,' said the priest.

Its homely smell seemed to settle him down. He bent and smelled at the soup. Impulsively Annie lifted the spoon.

'Would you like to taste it, Father?' she asked, and then she caught the bowl and held it out to him. 'Why don't you have it all, Father? I don't really want it. Do, do,' she said.

Unexpectedly the wardsmaid spoke. 'I could get more,' she said.

'No, no,' Father Patton cried. 'I was only curious to see what it was like.' He turned to Annie. 'You know the kind of muck I get thrown up to me in the parochial house!' Taking the spoon however he stirred about among the coarse-cut greens that floated in the soup. 'What's it called?' he asked.

No longer frightened of him, the girl giggled.

'Cocky-leaky, Father,' she said.

Instantly the priest let go the spoon, which fell back into the soup-plate, splashing the soup over the sheets.

'That's enough out of you!' he cried. And catching the girl by the arm he pushed her out of the room. 'Did you hear that?' he demanded of Annie. 'You'd

G

think butter wouldn't melt in her mouth, and then she comes out with the smut. Oh, I know her kind! and I know how I drew it down on me. It was mentioning her ugly stumps of legs that did it. They're all the same. They think that's all you're interested in! But she was wrong for once. Whatever else I may be, I'm not that kind! I didn't fail in *that* respect!'

Then, out of nowhere, an erratic gust of confidence seemed to blow over him.

'Maybe I'll get a parish yet!' he cried, 'and maybe sooner than we think too.' To her astonishment, Annie thought he winked, but then she realised it had been only an involuntary twitch of his eyelid. 'Do you know what?' he said, ' . . . I'm glad I came!' Visibly now, minute by minute, he was pulling himself together. 'You're not in as bad shape as I thought you'd be. You could be a lot worse. You'll see – things will work out somehow. Wait till you get home. One thing nobody seems to realise is that when you get home again you won't need as much money as before – you won't have the same chance to spend it, for one thing – and you won't be able to run about looking for ways of doing so either! The mistake all old people make is thinking that their needs will always be the same. You'll manage: you'll make out!' He came nearer. 'Let me give you a piece of advice. Don't let that brother of yours off too lightly. I've been making enquiries. Wasn't it you reared him? Has he no gratitude? I was told you used to be seen around the town, and you only a child, with him in your arms, when you ought to have been out enjoying yourself, courting and the like. He must have a short memory. You may not be able to make him pay the bill, but he ought at least to help out after you go home. Independence is all very well, but it can have its bad side too. Does it occur to you that you may be doing him great harm by letting him sneak out of his obligations? Oh, you didn't think of that! Well, it's time you did. I heard a friend of mine – another priest – talking along those lines some time ago, and he claimed that if you let people turn their back on the aged and the infirm, the next thing they'll want is to get rid of them altogether. Euthanasia! The same thing as is being done every other day up in the cats' and dogs' home in Dublin: putting the poor unwanted things to sleep – by scientific means, of course, only it's no different from the old way we all did it – putting them into a sack with a big stone at the bottom, and throwing it in the water butt!'

But Annie put her hands over her ears.

'Oh please, Father, please!' she cried, and then she took down her hands and her eyes flashed at him. 'I think you'd better leave,' she said.

'What's that?' As suddenly as the ranting began, it stopped. What did she mean? Hadn't she sent for him? What had changed her mind?

For the first time since he came into the room, he really looked at her. Was it because she was a woman? That seemed the only possible explanation.

Old as she was, and past it all – her flesh sagging –

she was a woman all the same. He didn't know much about women. Were their minds as private as their bodies? In the seminary as a student he was supposed to know as much about women as doctors did, but only from text books, charts, and diagrams. And after he was ordained he didn't trouble any more about them. He had written them off: it was easier that way. But suddenly, where once he used to think sex was the only difference between a man and a woman, it seemed, now, that maybe it was the only thing they had in common. He found himself thinking back to one day when he was nine or ten. Someone told him how his mother had carried him inside her before he was born, and at the thought of something moving in the stomach – something soft and slimy like frog-spawn, he supposed – he'd felt so queer he'd gone out to the coal-shed and been sick.

'Are you feeling all right, Father?' Annie was stretching out to him with her hands, trying to reach him. He drew back. With an effort he recalled that she had just said she was sorry she'd asked him to come to see her.

'What are you going to do?' he asked.

'I don't know!' Annie said. 'I'll have to think. I'll stay here till the end of the week anyway.' As if she was worn-out, she leant back against the head-board, and her doing so had a touch of finality to it. 'A week is a long time!' she said in a low voice. 'Anything could happen.'

Father Patton raised his heavy eyelids. Could she be

ailing from something other than the fall? She'd
failed a lot: he saw that now. Inside him, a horrible
hope leaped to life. He couldn't smother it, but he
knew he had to hide it.

'You might win the Sweep, is that it?' he said, and
the jaunty words made him feel so much better that a
real solution occurred to him: an immediate one.
'Couldn't they give you a job here in the hospital?
Wheeling around the meal-trolleys, maybe, or something like that?' But he'd forgotten her injury, and
the stick. 'Well, they might find something for you?'
he added lamely.

Annie shook her head. 'Don't worry about me,
Father,' she said. 'You've other things to worry about.'

What did she mean by that? Was she going to take
advantage of his having let her see he'd been upset?
Just in case, he would cut her down.

'You're over-reaching yourself I think,' he said.

But she looked back at him with a steady eye.

'Am I?' she said.

Outside the door there was again a sound of
crockery rattling.

'They're coming with more of their muck,' the
priest said.

'Yes,' said Annie. 'You'd better be going, Father.'

When he got outside the door of Annie's room,
Father Patton mopped at the sweat that had again
broken out on his forehead. Then a faint chill of ether
penetrated his nostrils. He kept the handkerchief to his

face as he went down the corridor towards the stairs. Through the large windows on the landing he saw that outside the rain had ceased and a high wind was shaking the trees in the park across the street.

Anxious to get out in the fresh air, he almost ran down the stairs, and when, on a lower landing, he met another wardsmaid coming up the stairs against him with a tray, he would have crashed into her if she hadn't flattened herself to the wall. Lazy sluts – still only bringing around the soup, he thought. Then he stopped short.

'What is the name of that soup?' he demanded roughly, not caring that he'd nearly frightened the girl out of her wits.

'Cocky-leaky, Father,' she whispered.

Taken aback, he caught her arm, spilling the soup. He looked around to see if the other wardsmaid was anywhere in sight. The corridor was empty: there could have been no collusion.

'What sort of a name is that for a soup?' he asked less crossly.

'I don't know, Father,' she said. 'We have it once a week.'

Father Patton stared at her. For some reason he felt better. But why?

Leaving the girl to stare after him, he went down the last flight of the stairs, and strode along the bottom corridor until in front of him he saw the glass doors through which he had entered the building. He pushed open the door and went out on to the steps.

The air was fresh against his face. A cold sun was trying to struggle through the clouds, but in the wind its pale light was blown about like candleflame.

He stood on the steps for a moment, looking across the street into the park. Over there everything was stirring, the leaves, the thin branches near the tops of the trees; and now and then a heavy branch swayed. And when a sudden flock of sparrows rose into the air he laughed to see how the high wind blew them about like leaves. But all this movement made him feel light-headed.

Carefully he went down the steps. Reaching the pavement he stopped again. All the movement in the sky was reflected in the wet pavement so that it seemed as if the world was upside down, and that it was the heavens, and not the earth, was underfoot.

Slowly he went over to the edge of the kerb where he had parked his car. He came to a stop again. At sight of the car he shuddered. It was so old, so dented, so pockmarked with rust; it was like a car you'd see abandoned in a back street, the tyres off, the upholstery ripped open, the springs and the padding protruding like guts. He could almost get the smell of it from where he stood: a smell of stale cigarette butts and sweaty feet. He couldn't bring himself to get into it. Rotten poky box of a car! He shook his fist at it.

'Box!' he shouted out loud. 'Box! Box!' But when some children playing in the street laughed, he moved hurriedly away, and having no particular place to go, he crossed the street and went into the park.

His life had been all boxes, he thought. First there was that box of a cubicle in the seminary. In it he was more awkward than most, being bigger boned than most. After that it was box after box; nothing but boxes: confessional boxes, poor boxes, collection boxes, and pamphlet boxes. Even God was kept in a box, shut up and locked into one. What else was the Tabernacle but only a box?

With the shock of this last thought, Father Patton came to a halt, and looking up he saw that he was standing under a tree covered along its sooty branches with young green leaves. He put up his hand impulsively and broke off a branch. He only wanted to look more closely at the tender young leaves; but there was something shocking about the white inner skin of the wood that was bared. Yet at the same time, the splintering sound of the breaking branch made him feel good. He broke a second little branch, and after a moment another, and suddenly he knew why the sound had made him feel good. He looked around the park with its pattern of paths leading one to a little glade, one to a fountain, one to a bandstand, and one to an ornamental lake on which he could see swans gliding freely and serenely. He would watch those swans for a start. After that, perhaps he'd go back to see Annie again, because . . .

But for the moment it was enough to be there in the park. Around him, like the sparrows, people were appearing from all sides to enjoy the unexpected sunlight.

The Lost Child

Leaving Mike to park the car, Renée got out and ran up the steps of the church, Iris could give a hand with the children. As long as she'd come, she might as well be put to use. She herself was entitled to a little separateness after that nerve-racking drive up to town with them all gabbling away unconcernedly about matters totally unrelated to the ceremony. Iris of course had been sceptical from the start, and Mike most probably thought it a pity she hadn't taken the step years ago and saved everyone a lot of misery. Well, it was her soul, not theirs.

But she had reached the porch, and without waiting to take holy water, she pushed open the baize-lined doors and went into the dark interior. Oh, the peace of that vast empty place of God. She closed her eyes. Enough to have reached it, she thought, when, behind her, she heard Iris and the children: Iris clumsily trying to push open the baize doors without letting go the hands of her niece and nephew.

'Where do we go, Renée?' Iris whispered. 'Do we stay with you?'

Renée trembled with annoyance. 'I haven't the least idea,' she said. It wasn't as if this was the first time her sister had set foot in a Catholic church.

But Iris was not to be put off.

'I suppose we may as well go down to the front,' she said, and she gave Renée a nudge to go forward.

Renée drew into herself. 'Why don't you wait for Mike?' she said, and this time there was such an edge on her voice it cut her free again, and Iris let her go. Detached completely, she started down the aisle alone, as if she were a bride. And then halfway down, inside the altar rail she saw a single prie-dieu that could only be for her. At the same time the sacristan stuck his head out of the sacristy door and gave a signal – not to the choir of course – but just as punctual as a peal from the organ Father Hugh stepped out on to the altar, ready and robed to receive her, his Ritual in his hand. After genuflecting smartly before the Tabernacle, Father Hugh turned and smiled at her, and opening the brass gate in the altar rail, he beckoned her to pass inside. He motioned to her to kneel on the prie-dieu. Nothing could have been more simple or yet more solemn, but apparently now Mike had joined Iris and the children, because behind her once more Renée heard them all coming down the aisle, the adults on tiptoe, their shoes creaking, and the children's feet clattering. She deliberately closed her eyes and waited till they got themselves into a pew. But why had they felt obliged to plank themselves down in the very front row? For there they were – she couldn't resist a glance back – sitting all strung out in a row like birds on a clothes line – although when he saw her looking back,

Mike got down on his knees at once, and made the children follow suit. Iris didn't budge, though: she evidently intended to stick to her guns and remain seated throughout. On all their faces – even on Iris's face – there was such a look of expectancy that Renée suddenly felt foolish. What did they expect?

Yet even she herself was surprised at how quickly the ceremony was over. She had been received into the Church!

Replacing the silk marker in his Ritual, Father Hugh shook hands with her in the most ordinary manner. Then he opened the brass gate again and preceded her down into the body of the church. There he shook hands warmly with her family, beginning of course with Mike, then the children, and then – with a slightly exaggerated warmth – with Iris.

Ought he to be asked to lunch? Renée wondered, but said nothing. Apparently Mike did not think it necessary; he just gave Father Hugh a nod and stood up to let his wife into the pew. He and Father Hugh were old friends.

'Move up there, children, and let your mother kneel down,' he said out loud as if they were not in a church at all. 'Goodbye Hugh,' he said, also out loud. 'We'll see you during the week, I suppose?'

'That's right,' said Father Hugh, and with a smile that embraced them all, he went back through the brass gate, shutting it carefully after him. Then, genuflecting in front of the altar he went into the sacristy with the quick impatient steps of one on familiar territory.

For a few minutes they all remained on their knees except Iris. Iris was examining the mortuary plaques on the wall. She looked bored. Renée turned and looked at the children. The expectancy was gone from their faces too. For them the ceremony had probably been a bit of a frost.

To recollect her thoughts, Renée would have liked to cup her face in her hands, but since this was a gesture reserved by born Catholics for the moments after Communion, she was afraid it would seem over-enthusiastic. It might annoy Mike. In spite of his wish that she should become a Catholic before they married, he had afterwards settled down to the idea of her never turning, and indeed, secretly he distrusted converts. It was incredible really to think how stubbornly she *had* resisted this step which in the end she had so willingly, so eagerly taken. For although at no time had she been prepared to lose Mike rather than give way, she'd gone very near to it once or twice. That was because of the hullaballoo his mother had made. Not that her own mother had been much better because when she herself finally consented to a Catholic wedding her mother behaved very badly.

'What on earth do you mean, Renée? You can't mean it will be held in the sacristy – the actual ceremony?' Her mother was outraged. 'How can you tolerate that? How can you allow your marriage to be a hole and corner business – it's an insult to your parents and your friends as well as to yourself. As for the slight cast on Iris – that is the worst of all.'

'Oh, I don't mind, Mother,' said Iris. 'It's just that I don't understand; that's all. What does my religion matter? I'd only be a witness.'

Their mother was somewhat placated.

'Anyway Iris you don't want to be a bridesmaid again, do you?' she said. 'You know the old saying, three times a bridesmaid never a bride.'

It was then Iris had said a very odd thing.

'Everyone doesn't set the same value on being a bride,' she said. 'I'm content never to marry if I don't meet a man of my own kind.'

She might as well have struck Renée between the eyes. And she knew it.

'Don't mind me, Renée,' she said. 'I'm jealous, that's all.' And she ran over and gave her a hug.

But her explanation simply didn't wash because Iris was the beauty of the family: she could have had anyone she wanted; she had any number of men, always. No one could understand why she didn't marry. If she was disturbed about the marriage it could only be supposed she was bigoted, because she was fond enough of Mike.

It was Iris who, in the end, spoke to their mother and told her the mistake she'd be making if she took any more risks with Mike. Their mother respected Iris. And on the day of the wedding it was their mother who impressed everyone by being briefed-up on procedure, not only genuflecting but making the sign of the cross as well.

'There!' she seemed to say, flashing an eye at the

in-laws. 'That is the behaviour I expect from people.'
Iris of course had needed no briefing, having been at
school in a convent in Belgium. She was a past master
at dabbling her fingers in holy water, and passing it on,
continental style, to her neighbours. As well as that
she had met Father Hugh and got on so well with him
she felt better about everything. Really the wedding
went off remarkably well, and it hadn't been in the
sacristy after all but in a side chapel.

When they came back from their honeymoon though,
and her mother came to visit, she barely concealed her
contempt when Renée served fish on Friday. And
later she nearly hit the ceiling when she heard her
grandchild – Babette – was to be baptised a Catholic.

'But I promised, Mother; You know that!'

'I only know that such a promise should never have
been extracted,' said her mother. 'It was given under
duress – emotional duress.'

'Oh, give over, Mother, will you?' she cried. 'Do
you want us to be happy or do you not? Can't you see
I'm only doing it to make things easier for Mike?'

'Why can't he make things easier for you?'

'Well, for one thing,' she flashed, '*his* mother would
make life worse for him than you're trying to make it
for me. And in any case, Mike is bound under pain
of mortal sin in this.'

Her mother gave her a scathing look. 'And you are
willing to let your children grow up in the same
bonds?'

'Oh Mother, please, please,' she said wearily. 'You

don't understand, that's all. I care more about Mike than I do about any church – his or mine.'

To give her mother her due, that silenced her. As for Iris, by then she had met so many priests in their house – most of them had been at school or college with Mike – and she'd got on so famously with them, it began to look as if it would be she who would turn, and not Renée. All the same they had had one bitter argument after Renée had started to receive instruction. They had gone to Achill on one of their week-end trips, and Iris had gone with them. They were staying in a small hotel close to the shore, and they had gone for a stroll along Dugort Strand after putting the children to bed. As they walked along the shore they had to pick their steps, because the tufty shore-grass was dotted with half-concealed stones and they could easily trip and twist an ankle. Suddenly Iris stopped.

'I thought the rocks along here were all part of a natural formation,' she said, 'but look – surely there is some attempt at pattern in this?'

Mike and Renée stopped too and looked where she pointed. It did seem there was a regularity in the disposition of the small rocks at their feet – some forty or fifty at least. There was no cutting or marking on them and yet they seemed to have been set down deliberately by the hand of man.

'Let's see if the guide book has anything to say about them,' said Mike, taking it out of his pocket. 'You're right, Iris,' he said, commending her. He looked around him to take his bearing from the overhanging cliffs and then turned to calculate the distance from a small pier to the left of where they stood. 'This must be it . . .' he said, 'it's indicated on the map too. And it has a name – Cillin na Leanbh – the Cemetery of the Children.' He looked happily at Renée. 'I bet there aren't many people who spot this!' He was too pleased with himself to see there was anything wrong with Iris: on the contrary he patted her on the arm. 'Weren't you smart, Iris. Only for you we would have passed by and not noticed!'

Renée however had sensed trouble. Iris was staring around her at the bleak shore, so lonely, with not a soul in sight.

'Why did they bury them here? Why not in the ordinary cemetery down in the village?'

The harsh air had reddened her face but that was not enough to account for her excited look. Renée did not know what could be wrong, but she felt uneasy.

'It's much more beautiful up here anyway,' she cried, hoping to dismiss the matter. And she began to walk on. In any case, she herself had had enough of the place. There was something odd and disturbing about it. But Iris stood stubbornly where she was and looked not at Mike but at her sister.

'It's certainly beautiful, but that's hardly the reason for the choice,' she said.

What was she driving at? Did she suspect some kind of superstition which she attributed not to the ignorance of a peasant community but to their barbarous religion?

'Is it because they were illegitimate?' Iris asked then, and there was such a note of fierceness in her voice that at last Mike realised there was something wrong.

'Certainly not,' he replied. 'The Church does not discriminate in such cases as long as the child is baptised.' His voice was vibrant with self-righteousness. 'I've never seen one of these places before,' he said, 'but I believe they were common at one time, and there are some in other parts of the country.' Confident that he had stamped out his sister-in-law's spark of rebellion, he turned to take his wife's arm with the intention of comfortably walking on when Renée pulled away.

'But that's inhuman,' she said. 'How must the poor mother have felt?'

'Don't mind the mothers,' Iris cried. 'How would *anyone* feel – any *proper* person?' Unconsciously the sisters drew together.

Against them Mike stood at bay. Then, although they knew he detested crudity of any kind, the two women started at what he said next.

'It's no worse than what is done every other day in hospitals and nursing homes.'

'And what is that?' It was Renée who had asked, and in a whisper.

Mike shrugged his shoulders. 'How do I know?' he said harshly, 'but I'm pretty sure they don't hold a full funeral for a foetus.'

'Oh Mike! That *word*!' It made her feel sick, and he

H

knew she loathed it. He must be very upset. She looked out over the sea where a last cold glitter of light came from under the clouds. It might easily rain. 'Oh, come on – let's not talk about it any more,' she said. 'The custom is obsolete anyway.' Warning Iris with a look, she began to walk back to the hotel.

But one morning in the following week, when they were home, Iris drove up in her car; the tyres screeching on the gravel. She marched into the house, holding up the handbook of the Antiquarian Society.

'Listen to this,' she commanded.

'Immediately on the cliff edge at the east end of Dugort Strand a number of small rough and uninscribed slabs are to be seen. This spot is locally called Cillin na Leanbh. In this spot are buried the bodies of unbaptised children, and a rough slab is erected over each. There is no enclosing wall and the grave slabs are only just visible through the heather. The custom of burying unbaptised infants on useless pieces of ground like the present site was formerly common throughout the whole country but . . .'

Here she paused dramatically, and, leaving down the handbook on the table, she quoted the rest from memory,

'but to a large extent the custom has now ceased.'

To a large extent. Do you hear that? In other words, it has not ceased: it is not obsolete. Oh Renée, are you prepared to accept things like that?'

Renée was in fact shocked but she found Iris inter-

fering. 'I'll take it up with Father Hugh,' she said,
and, having said that, she felt no obligation to listen
to ranting from Iris.

Father Hugh, however, needed no new issue to
come up in order to urge her to go slow about a final
decision. That was one of the things that surprised
her; the thoroughness of her instruction: it amounted
almost to unwillingness on the part of the priest to
receive her into the Church at all.

'What is the hurry?' he asked smiling. 'Your faith
will be all the stronger if it comes as a result of living
with a good Catholic man like Mike.'

'What if it's the other way round?' she asked,
unable to resist the quip.

'Fair enough!' said the priest, and he laughed out-
right. And although at the time her Protestant probity
resented what she felt to be an attempt to ingratiate
himself with her, yet she knew he was incapable of
duplicity. It was just that, like his Church, he believed
so staunchly in male superiority, he could not concede
the possibility of the woman having the stronger pull
in matters of the mind.

And yet, in the end, it was the maleness of the
Church that had, as Mike put it, hooked her. She could
lean on it.

'Or is that a silly way to put it, Father Hugh?' she
asked one day.

'My dear,' he said, 'have you never seen how, in
pictures of the Good Shepherd, the lost lamb leans
against Jesus – trusts himself to Those Arms? I think

you have expressed yourself very beautifully. We Catholics do lean on our Church.'

That somehow settled it. And here she now was within the Church, having entrusted her full weight to it. But suddenly, with a start, she realised she had not said one prayer, had not offered one word of gratitude to God for the grace that had been bestowed on her. Yet she must have been on her knees for ages. The others were getting restless; the children were beginning to bicker wordlessly. Babette was pulling her brother's handkerchief from him, using her strength meanly, letting him think he was getting it one minute, and then tugging it away. She could easily pull him off the edge of the pew on to the floor. What a howl he'd give then! Renée realised she'd have to be content with one quick prayer. First however she glanced at Mike. She couldn't help noticing that he looked subdued. The children too in spite of their bickering had a subdued look. Poor little things, for them the ceremony was probably a disappointment. The solemnity of their own First Communion Day was still fresh in their minds, with the feasting afterwards, the sugar kisses and silver-papered presents from friends and relatives. Even Iris looked disappointed, having her own memories, no doubt, of their convent days in Courtrai where even the Protestant boarders shared in the First Communion goodies, amassing heaps of iced almonds – virgin white and tasting as sweet as scent – to make caches against the lesser, leaner days of the calendar.

Oh, those years in Courtrai. To think she had lived under the same roof with the Blessed Sacrament and had been so indifferent to it. A sharp nostalgia for those bygone days made her throw an arm around Babette.

Taking this to be an end to praying, the child whispered to her:

'What are we going to do next?'

'Have lunch,' said Mike, overhearing her. He sat up and began to dust his knees. 'We may as well get out of here, hadn't we?' he said, in what would have seemed an irreverent tone if it weren't for the devout way he was making the sign of the cross at the same time. 'Are you ready, Renée?' he said quite roughly for him, but she understood him. Distrusting the convert, he was afraid she'd expect to stay there half the day. So, with one piercing look at the Tabernacle, suffused with joy, she too got to her feet. In the aisle she took care to genuflect quickly, and as if carelessly, like a born Catholic.

When they reached the door, a bit dazed she was about to step out into the sunlight, forgetting to take holy water, till Iris stretched out her hand. Then, hastily dipping into the font she passed a damp touch to Iris in the continental manner. Poor Iris – little things like that made the whole thing more palatable to her. Renée wondered why, in fact, her sister had come with them to the church. It must have been out of regard for the children: to help make it an occasion for them. Renée's heart smote her again:

they must all feel very let down. In addition they were probably hungry: it was past noon. She herself was not hungry but she did feel very tired. She wished that they were going home to spend the rest of the day normally. She turned to Mike, but it was hard to see what was in his mind. He wouldn't be human if he wasn't thinking it a pity his mother had not lived to see this day. Yet she herself could not truthfully regret the old woman's absence: her satisfaction would have been so tactlessly evident, the ceremony would have been more objectionable for Iris.

'It was nice of you to come, Iris,' she whispered impulsively, giving her sister's arm a squeeze as they went down the steps.

'Oh, not at all,' said Iris. 'I thought it would be expected of me.'

'Do you mind awfully?'

'Why should I?' her sister said. 'It's entirely your concern.' But something in her voice struck Renée as odd, and she looked enquiringly at her. What reservations did she still have? 'What is the matter, Iris?' she asked, putting all the warmth she could into her voice, because now she was very, very tired.

But Mike was all for moving off.

'Where are we going to eat?' he asked, and unconsciously with his hand he felt inside his jacket to make sure he had his wallet. That always meant he had planned an extra-good meal.

'Where would you like to go, Iris?' Renée asked, anxious to give her sister the choice.

'Oh, anywhere suits me,' said Iris. 'Oughtn't *you* to have the choice? Sort of like long ago when one was the Birthday Girl!'

They all laughed at that, the children loudly and noisily.

'Well, the Birthday Girl has no preferences,' Renée said truthfully. Then she hesitated and turned to Mike. 'Perhaps not an oriental restaurant though, on account of the garlic.'

'But I thought you *loved* garlic?' Iris was astonished.

'Oh!' said Renée, and stopped dead. She blushed and dropped her voice. 'Didn't you know – didn't I tell you. . . ? We're going to have another child. I meant to tell you but I kept forgetting: it seems so far off – it won't be till October – nearly November.'

As Iris said absolutely nothing even Mike got nervous and broke in. 'We're not even sure yet.'

Renée smiled gratefully at him. 'That's right. We could easily be mistaken,' she said, 'although I don't think so.' Then she laughed. 'We could put it to the test, of course, by going to an Indian restaurant, because one smell of garlic turns me inside out – in the early stages anyway.'

Iris missed the joke. Her face had become deadly serious.

'We most certainly won't go anywhere that would upset you, Renée,' she cried.

'Oh, I was exaggerating,' said Renée: she disliked the solicitous note in her sister's voice. If there was one thing she would hate more than another at this moment it would be an obstetrical chat. Hoping to deflect her sister's interest in her, she reached back into the conversation and tried to salvage the topic she had a few minutes before allowed to founder. 'Was it an awful ordeal for you, Iris? The ceremony I mean?'

'Oh no,' said Iris. 'I always knew from the moment you married him that you'd turn one day. But I must say that now . . .' She paused. ' . . . and only in view of what you've just told me I am worried. I wouldn't have thought *now* the most appropriate time for making decisions – of any kind.'

'Well, really!' Renée was so taken aback she gasped. 'You don't mean because of my condition? – you *can't* mean that? That it has clouded my judgment! After all, I've been in this condition on two other occasions and I didn't change my religion. Oh Iris, you fall so short of understanding.'

But Iris looked her straight in the eyes.

'That's right, I do,' she said, and catching Babette's hand she bent down and gave the child her full attention. 'Where would *you* like best to go?' she asked.

Never having expected to be given the choice, both children nevertheless were ready with an answer.

'The Zoo!' they cried. 'The Zoo!'

Renée could have shaken her sister. The Zoo was out of the question. Better an oriental restaurant, garlic and all, than the Zoo. Out of her depth, she flashed an appeal for help to Mike.

'Think of the smell in the Lion House!' she said. 'I couldn't stand it.'

The damage was done though. Babette was pouting. She had been angelic, up to now, but who dare dash the hopes of an angel?

'Why can't we go to the Zoo?' the child demanded.

They all came to a stand.

'Because this is your mother's day,' said Mike. 'It's her, not you, who is to be considered.'

'Why did you ask us, so?' Babette took her hand away from Iris and caught the hand of her small brother.

Behind the children, Iris was making signs, and silently forming words with her lips. Renée was unreasonably irritated.

'What are you trying to say?' she asked out loud.

Betrayed, Iris flushed. 'I only wondered if they knew.'

'No, they don't,' Renée snapped. 'But perhaps it's time they did.' She was almost frightened by how tired she felt now.

Mike raised his eyebrows. 'Isn't it a bit early to tell them? They'd get an awful let-down if it was a false alarm.'

But the children had got wind that there was something concealed from them.

'Oh, what is it? Tell us!' they cried. Feeling certain they would be told, their sulks gave way to excited anticipation and they began to hop like hailstones on the pavement.

'Tell them, Mike,' said Renée.

'I suppose we may as well,' said Mike, and then as

the children clutched him and rocked him from side to side, their excitement became contagious and his face broke out in the first real smile of the morning. 'Your mother has been planning a surprise for you,' he began . . .

But Renée intervened. 'It's not something specially for them,' she said. 'Don't raise their hopes too much. It won't be arriving till – '

'Oh, Mummy!'

Stunned by joy, the children stopped hopping up and down. And after the one exclamation they fell so silent Renée laughed. Then she realised she must seize her advantage *now*.

'So you see – about going to the Zoo . . .' she began, but Babette needed no explanations.

'Oh, but of course, Mummy, you must do what you want.' And then, more prescient than anyone could have supposed, she ran over and whispered in her ear: 'Why don't you go home, Mummy, and lie down. We'd be good. And you'd get a rest from us.'

'Would you like to do that, Renée?' Mike asked, partly surprised, partly relieved. 'You would!' he cried, answering for her. 'I think it's a very good idea,' he added. 'Look, let's do it in style. Let's send you home by taxi: it's not extravagant: it won't cost more than your share of the meal! You look deadly tired.' He turned to the others. 'Here – let's put her into a taxi right now.' And from a hackney rank just opposite them he hailed a cab.

A wonderful feeling of being minded came over

Renée as Mike put her into the taxi. As she sank back
on the seat she saw that Mike, himself, was delighted
with the way he'd handled things. Only as the taxi
moved off did she think of Iris. She wound down the
window. 'What about you, Iris? Will you be all
right?'

Iris didn't hear but by the look on her face it seemed
that she was taking things good-humouredly. Anyway,
Renée didn't care. She leaned back again and closed
her eyes, prepared to give way to utter exhaustion.
But as the taxi gathered speed she found it irksome to
keep her eyes closed. She sat up. Was it possible that
she wasn't tired at all, only anxious to be alone? In
fact she felt lively and full of energy. She really ought
to have gone by bus: the exercise would have been
good. She smiled to herself thinking how Mike had
treated her as if she were made of glass when she was
expecting Babette, or at least had tried to do so until
she showed him what it said about exercise in her
manual on childbirth.

How she swore by that manual during her first
pregnancy, and even her second. This time she hadn't
consulted it once.

'You've got the knack, old girl,' Mike said laughing.
But he had been impressed all the same by the way
she'd read up about childbirth. As a business man he
felt that this was because she was a University graduate.
He was always telling people how she learned to drive
the car from a handbook on driving, and how, when
they inherited the farm, she had read up on compost

and animal genetics until she knew more about farming than him, although he'd been born and brought up on a farm. 'She had her babies by the book too,' he'd add beaming, and he felt sure that was why they were so strong and healthy and yet fine-boned. He was very proud of Babette's clear skin and her beautiful auburn hair, although he had misgivings about the boy's hair.

'It was all those carrots you ate,' he said, and privately Renée felt that perhaps she had overdone things where the boy was concerned; he was almost better-looking than Babette, but she had to defend her theories.

'Not at all. *Les carrottes pour faire rire,*' she said.

But thinking of this reminded her that she had intended to buy some lettuce when they were in town. In spite of owning a farm they often had to buy vegetables: it just didn't pay to grow them out of season. The taxi was turning into Thomas Street. Perhaps she could get some greens at one of the street barrows, but no, the vendors were all packing up and what was left was wilted and yellowing. Indeed, the refuse around the stalls was enough to put one off vegetables for life. The discarded outer leaves trodden into the ground, already rotting and giving off a stench, and the big stalks of cabbage and cauliflower that littered the street were disgusting, simply disgusting. She smiled. Lettuce always reminded her of the time Mike's younger brother called to tell them his wife was expecting her first baby, and poor Mike began recommending her to eat greens when his brother cut him short and said *his* wife was a healthy woman and didn't have to go in for food fads. How they laughed at the time, and indeed they laughed again later, but a little unkindly, when his pasty-faced progeny arrived.

She looked out. They had come to the end of Thomas Street and were turning down by St. Patrick's Hospital. Her last chance of getting lettuce was gone, but it was just as well: she'd forgotten that she'd have had to lug it across the fields. That was something they'd have to do in the coming summer – make a proper driveway into the house. Not that she ever regretted their having sited the house so far in from the road. But it had meant postponing the making of an avenue since nothing would satisfy Mike but tar macadam. In the summer they were able to get in and out easily, driving the car through the fields. And they chanced it occasionally on hard frosty days in winter too, but on a day like this – with a touch of spring in the air – the ground would be too soft. One could not ask a city taxi-man to risk it. Anyway the walk through the fields would be pleasant. It would give her an appetite, for although she was eating well enough, she wouldn't say she had quite the same eagerness for food that she had when she was carrying the other two children.

For the first time since she'd decided she was pregnant, Renée thought of her unborn child. What sex would it be, she wondered. She had read somewhere that it would soon be possible to determine the sex of a child before birth. It might even be possible to pre-determine it, but somehow she rejected the idea of this. She resented it, in fact, because it seemed that it would in some way interfere with the sense of power that one felt at carrying a living creature within one, feeding it from one's own bloodstream and sustaining its life-breath with one's own heart-pulse. But alas, it was not only the flesh of our flesh that we passed on to our children, but something of the mind too, and the character and even the personality. A shadow fell over Renée at the thought of all the unpleasant relatives whose traits it would positively pain her to pass on to her child. And yet the secret seeds of ancestry were already at work in her womb. Against such an un-pleasant thought she closed her eyes and leaned her head back on the leather cushions. An image formed in her mind of a broad stream, flowing strongly, but going against the current, like a salmon going up-stream to spawn, there was. . . .

She must have been asleep. The taxi had jolted to a stop and she opened her eyes, startled. The taxi-man following Mike's instructions had crossed the bridge over the Boyne, but finding no driveway on his right as he had expected, but only a gap with a pole across it leading in to what seemed a rutted cow-path, he had cruised on till he came to the cross-roads a couple of hundred yards beyond the farm.

'Oh, that was our entrance, that gap in the hedge!' Renée cried, but seeing the dismay on his face she laughed and assured him she didn't expect him to go down to the house. 'I'll get out here,' she said, 'and you can continue along this road. It will bring you out again to the main road, and be slightly shorter in fact.'

For her it meant a little longer walk, going through a small beechwood that divided their property from their neighbour's, but on a day like this it ought to be heaven in the woods. She got out and paid the taximan. But the man did not immediately drive away. Perhaps noticing her high heels, and remembering Mike's decidedly citified appearance, he was thinking it odd they lived so far from Dublin.

'Have you much land there?' he asked, with the innocent curiosity of a city man.

'Only a few acres,' she said, and she smiled at him. 'It's not a real farm – we just graze a few cattle – let them eat the grass,' she explained patiently as to a child, 'No cows, no pigs.'

He nodded, and after a last look over the fields he let in the clutch and began to move away. Standing back Renée waved at him, glad when he was gone, because it would have been awkward getting over the rickety fence into the wood. The fence was so shaky she had to jump down on the other side, high heels and all. Fortunately the ground was not as soft as she thought: there was a hard core in it after all. It was beautiful in the wood. Walking over the dried leaves between the trees she felt an increasing sense of well-being. Everywhere there was evidence that spring was on the way, although everywhere too there was evidence of the damage done by winter. There were two big trees blown down and several trees had branches broken. And when she came to the edge of the wood and looked out at the fields, she noticed as never before how winter had flattened the grass. In places it was so bare it was more like a lawn than a pasture. And what was here? She stopped. In the middle of the field was the huge stone that she and Mike had let fall from the tractor one day last summer. They had been drawing stones for a dry-wall they were building at the end of the garden. They had the loan of the tractor, and they had a neighbour's young son to help them load it, but this big stone rolled off after the boy had left them and gone home to milk, and it was too heavy for them to lift alone. Every week they meant to fetch it but when the wall was finished without it, they forgot about it. Soon the grass grew over and hid it from sight. Now it was uncovered again. She went over to it. It was huge, and she saw now that it was roughly chiselled, perhaps by one of the old monks to whom the land once belonged. It would have been a pity to have buried it in a wall: it would be marvellous as a feature in the garden, a focal point, with bulbs planted around it. But it would be an awful job to move it. It had sunk into the ground and was netted down with couch grass. Still, it ought to be possible to lever it up and by means of a plank roll it into a wheel-barrow. With the toe of her shoe she prodded it, but it didn't stir; it was as firmly rooted as a tree. Yet, the thought of salvaging it excited her, and walking on, she found herself stepping out faster. And, planning where she'd place it, her mind, too, was soon racing.

At last she reached the gable end of the house, and there, in the warm border under the wall she saw that several crocuses had thrust up their green tips, but – she went closer and then she laughed out loud – two or three of them, more than that – four, five – oh, lots and lots – had thrust upwards in such a frenzy of growth they had shot out of the ground altogether and lay upended on top of the clay. She'd have to put them back. She'd have to get a trowel. Or she could push them back with her fingers – make a hole perhaps with her heel. No, better do it properly.

Eager to get into the house and change her clothes and be out again using up all the energy surging through her, she hurried around to the front door. It was extraordinary how everywhere, simply every-where she looked, there were things to be done, which, blinkered by winter, she had not noticed. And when she got to the door and put her key in the lock, right beside the door, she saw something else that would have to be done at once – oh, but at once. Her precious, precious old rose Gloire de Dijon – whose young shoots had prematurely put out spurts of tender green leaf in the shelter of the wall, was blasted by frost. If the blackened tips were not cut off imme-diately the whole shoot would die – the whole bush. Without going into the house, Renée hurried around to the potting shed and got the pruning shears. It would

I

only take a few minutes to attend to it, she thought.

Half an hour later she was still hacking away at the bush. There was more damage done than she'd thought. And from the Gloire de Dijon she'd gone on to inspect the Madame Alfred Carrière on the terrace. This too had dead shoots. Less rare than the Dijon but more beautiful, this was an older and larger bush that she'd transplanted from their former garden, and once she'd tackled this she'd let herself in for a really tiresome job. When at last she'd finished, she sat down on a stone seat to rest before going inside and getting something to eat. She certainly had an appetite now. She was famished.

A few minutes after she'd gone inside and made the tea, she was about to put it on a tray and take it up to her room, when she happened to look out of the kitchen window. What did she see at the end of the garden but the long expected load of manure! It had arrived while they were away. Almost knocking over the tea in her excitement, she ran to the window. Not having stall-feds they had to depend on local farmers for manure for the garden. This involved an endless humiliation of begging and an endless annoyance of broken promises, because although to her manure was something money could not buy, the farmers felt they were only humouring her by giving it. It was always when she'd given up hope of getting it that a tractor would roll up with a load. Or else, like now, she'd come back from town to find a load dumped down anywhere.

What a place it had been dumped today! If only she'd been at home. Why on the lawn? It was down at the end of the garden, of course, but it would ruin the grass, burn it to the roots. And so near the herbaceous border! She opened the window and looked out. How awful – a lot had toppled down into the border. That would have to be taken away immediately. But by whom? She didn't have the car to go looking for a man to do it, and it was unlikely that she could persuade anyone to spare a man on such a fine day. Perhaps there wasn't as much damage done as she thought? Putting down her cup she ran out.

It was pretty bad: the big heap of manure, still steaming in places, had been thrown down so carelessly that one whole side had collapsed and flowed like lava into the flower bed. It had entirely engulfed the smaller plants, and lots of the larger plants further back were up to their necks in it.

She could have cried. It had almost smothered her beautiful Chinese peonies that were due to flower for the first time this summer, their leaf buds already unfurling. Trembling with annoyance Renée ran back to the tool house and got a fork – just a garden fork. She could never handle the big five-pronged fork which a man would use, and with which short work would have been made of the job. Oh, if only Mike was home! But they'd hardly be back till dark. Damn Iris! she thought unreasonably, as if all this was in some way her sister's fault. Catching up the fork she set to work.

To clear the manure from the peonies was not such a big job after all. She used her hands most of the time and it wasn't long until she'd freed the peonies and also a bush of sandalwood and several lavender bushes. The smaller plants were a different matter. On them the dung lay in such thick wet slabs it was hard to fork it off, and after that, fling it to the back of the border where there were bare spaces between the shrubs. It was no joke but she got through it and had just heaved a sigh and decided to stop when she noticed that the main heap was still top-heavy. Unless a few forkfuls were taken off the top, it could topple over again and her labour would be in vain. Taking a deep breath she set to work once more.

This was really heavy going. The dung, heavy with urine, had a dead weight and every time she dug the fork in, it let out an evil smell. Compared with compost it was very unpleasant. Her compost heap was a pride and a joy to her. She'd made it by the book too, putting everything into it, grass clippings, leaves, the tops of plants when they were cut down, everything. She often went out with the tea-strainer and threw the tea leaves on it. Mike used to laugh at her in the beginning, but he was impressed by the results. He'd plunge in his arm and bring out a fistful to show a visitor, opening his hand slowly to let the soil run out like sand between his fingers. It was amazing to think a mass of refuse and garden offal could turn back into sweet-smelling loam. So different from this filthy stuff that took so long to decompose. Yet, in the ground this too would be transformed. She took another deep breath and plunged the fork into it once more, raising – with an effort – another layer. But the next instant she let go the fork and put her hands over her mouth in disgust. Ugh. Under the hot coverlet a mess of worms snuggled. Stabbed with light, blindly and clumsily they began to uncoil. The sight was nauseating, but she kept her head, realising that if they crawled back into the darkness of the heap she would be liable to uncover one with every forkful, whereas now, if she gritted her teeth and acted fast, she might lift the whole disgusting posse of them and fling it out of her sight. Taking up the fork again she lunged it into the middle of the dung. But oh God, she'd bungled it; the creatures had already squirmed in every direction, twisting and turning and crawling over each other, and when the wad of dung was lifted one or two of the things tumbled over the side, almost falling into her shoe.

Sickened, she threw down the fork. But oh God, there was a worm impaled on one of the prongs. Utterly demoralised, her impulse was to run, but how could one – above all one in her condition – deny any creature – even a disgusting thing like that – its right to life! She'd *have* to free it. Putting her hand to her stomach, or she'd retch, she took up the fork for the third time and with her shoe tried to dislodge the writhing thing skewered to it. No use. Only her fingers could do it.

But after she'd freed it, oh God! the mangled

creature fell apart, dropping on to the ground in two parts. As if they had been in dirty water, Renée shook her hands before she thought of wiping them, and when she did, she wiped them frantically – on her skirt, on her sleeves, on her jumper, but all the time she watched the thing, unable to look away. *Both* parts of it were writhing – its entity doubled, its agony doubled. Oh God. Had it no part that could die?

Suddenly she screamed, and putting her hands over her face she started to run towards the house.

'Renée? What's wrong with you? Renée!'

It was Mike. They'd come home sooner than she expected. Mike took her in his arms.

'What were you at?' he cried. 'What's the matter with you – you look so queer.' Then he took in the situation. 'I thought it was to rest you came home,' he said angrily, although instinctively his arms had closed on her and he was stroking her hair. Crying hysterically, she could not speak. 'What made you tackle a heavy job like that? – at this time?' he said. She pulled away from him. She had to defend herself against *that*.

'You know we always agreed that there was no need to coddle oneself because of' – she sobbed again – 'one's condition. You've always gone along with me that work is no harm; it's only nervous exhaustion that hurts.' But she couldn't explain properly with the sobs and gulps that broke from her involuntarily, her words jerking out foolishly. 'You always said you were glad I didn't trade on my condition – to get out of my obligations. And this job was urgent.' She pounded him with her fists. 'You can't turn on me now! You've got to take the good with the bad. Oh, I never knew you were so mean. Before Babette was born – don't you remember – the nurse was going to get me to lift the bed – she said that in the maternity hospitals they always made the patients do that – lift the beds!' She looked up at him. She'd always been able to make him laugh by telling him that, but at that minute, Iris, whom she hadn't seen till then, took her by the arm and shook her.

'Yes – to induce labour!' Iris said, and Iris was furious too, her face white with anger. 'You were full term then – but in your present state there's no earthly excuse for taking risks. . . .'

Pushing Mike away, Renée turned on Iris.

'Are you trying to teach me my business?' she cried, enraged, but even in her distracted state she was appalled by the viciousness that underlay her words, and she wasn't really surprised when Iris burst into tears. 'Oh, why are you crying, Iris?' she asked imploringly, although suddenly she knew why: Iris was lonely. Now she understood what her sister meant by those odd words on the eve of the wedding. She hadn't meant that Mike was not of their persuasion; she'd meant that she, Renée, for fear of never finding love, had settled for marriage. 'It's not true, Iris,' she said, fending off an accusation, that had not been made.

Then, as if the whole world was made of crockery,

and she had let it fall, her ears were filled with sounds of clatter and breakage. Only the voice of her sister came through it talking to Mike.

'Let's get her up to bed,' said Iris, and one at each side of her they led her to the house, while the children – God help them – stared uncomprehendingly.

It was good to be in bed. There was a luxury in lying there while outside it was still daylight, and only the sleepy note in the throat of a bird gave indication that evening was approaching. And here came Iris, smiling and kind again, to take away her supper tray, and Mike with an early edition of the evening paper he'd bought on the way home and forgotten in the fuss.

'I don't deserve all this attention,' said Renée. 'I'm as fit as a fiddle. I just got worked up over those beastly worms. I feel marvellous.'

'That's good,' said Mike, but he looked anxiously at her and then at Iris. Uneasily Renée's own glance went from one to the other of them. 'You don't think I did myself any harm?' she asked, and then she clapped her hand to her mouth. 'I forgot something,' she said. 'Where is the book – the baby manual – there's something about going easy on certain days of the month and in the very early stages.' Her eyes filled with tears. 'Oh Mike,' she cried. 'How could I forget – it expressly stipulated – '

But Mike pushed her back on the pillow. 'There is only one thing expressly stipulated, and that is that you stop worrying, and try to go to sleep.'

'But it's still daylight.'

'Is it?' said Mike wearily, glancing out of the windows. 'No matter,' he said. 'When Iris gives the kids something to eat I'm coming to bed myself – although,' he said, turning his head to listen to sounds below, 'it may well be dark before that's accomplished – they've had a long day.' Then he corrected himself hastily. 'They've had a great day,' he said, 'but like all of us they're over-excited. Try to sleep, Renée. I'll be up as soon as I can.'

He did come up early – before ten certainly – but Renée had not slept, although she had not put on the light even when darkness fell. Filled with a curious peace, she lay back on the pillows and gradually the fatigue drained out of her. She had only to lie quiet, she felt, and her system would empty itself of all the tension that had been stored up for days. When Mike did come into the room she did not want to talk.

'Don't put on the light, Mike,' she called out, 'unless you want to read or something. I'll just run into the bathroom and we'll go right to sleep.'

'How do you feel now?' Mike asked.

'I feel fine,' she said, 'just fine,' and she ran into the bathroom that adjoined their room.

A minute later, standing on the cold tiles in the bathroom, she heard Mike's name called out and then called again, and with the strange cold sweat that had broken out all over her body she could not concentrate on who it was that was calling him.

'Mike. Mike. Mike.'

'For God's sake, what's the matter, Renée?' Mike cried, running in and turning on the light.

All she could do was point to the floor where, splashed on the white tiles, serrated like a star, there was a drop of bright red blood.

'I'm bleeding!'

'Oh, for God's sake,' Mike's voice rose, both relieved and cross at the same time. 'You gave me a fright.'

'But can't you see – it means there's something wrong,' she said desperately.

'Oh now, hold on to yourself, old girl,' said Mike. 'You're getting hysterical again.' He was referring to the worms, she supposed. But this was real.

'We'll have to call the doctor!'

'At this hour? For that! Have sense,' said Mike. Taking a towel he bent and wiped up the blood. Then he put an arm around her. 'Get back into bed,' he said. 'All the doctor would do is tell you to lie down and wait till morning. Come on, old girl, get into bed – you may never hear another word about this! One swallow doesn't make a summer you know . . . !' and as she didn't follow he put a hand under her chin. 'One drop of blood doesn't make a haemorrhage,' he said, trying to drag a smile from her. But she found the humour forced and heavy. And the word haemorrhage scared her.

'Do you mean a miscarriage?' she cried, her voice rising.

'Oh look here, Renée,' said Mike. 'Which of us is

the woman – you or me? You may not be pregnant at all!'

The surprise of this suggestion gave her a brief respite from panic. She laughed, and while she was laughing Mike led her back to their room. 'What a fool you'd look if you got the doctor out here for nothing,' he said. ' In the morning, if you like, you can ring him and have a check-up. You'd be having one anyway. I'm surprised you took it on yourself to be so sure of your condition – telling the kids and Iris – I suppose you were going by that blasted book.'

She had forgotten the book. 'You didn't get it for me when I asked you,' she said. 'Oh, run downstairs and get it, Mike, will you? It's in one of the drawers of my desk, somewhere at the back. You'll have to hunt for it, but I'd love to glance at it.'

'Oh, cut it out, will you?' said Mike. He switched on the light. 'You look marvellous. There couldn't be anything wrong. You looked bad in the garden – and ghastly there in the bathroom a minute ago, but you look great now. How do you feel – honestly?'

She had to admit she felt all right.

'Except that I'm a bit scared,' she hesitated, 'for the baby, I mean.'

'Oh nonsense,' said Mike. 'It will be a tough little beggar like the others.' Getting into bed he switched off the light, and in a second he was asleep. Lying beside him, a small seed of resentment in Renée's heart had no time to germinate because a second later she, too, was asleep.

It was towards daybreak, no, it was actually seven o'clock, although it still seemed dark outside, when she woke again. She got up and sat on the side of the bed with her feet dangling.

'Mike, will you ring him now?' she asked. 'I don't want to get out of bed, just in case.'

She had wakened in such full possession of her fears it was hard to realise that Mike did not know what she was talking about for a minute.

'Oh, that,' he said then. 'Are you still upset. . . ? It's damned early to ring any man, even a doctor, unless it's extremely urgent.'

'It is extremely urgent,' she said hotly. 'He might be going away or something.' That was the worst of living in the country and having to depend on one doctor. 'We've got to catch him before he makes his plans for the day.'

Mike sat up. That much at least!

'Maybe Iris would do it,' he said.

Renée stared. 'Did Iris stay the night? You didn't tell me?'

'I thought it might frighten you,' Mike said cautiously.

'Then you *were* worried?' she accused.

'Not about this nonsense,' Mike said wearily. 'We were worried at the state you'd got yourself into. . . .' But suddenly he looked anxious. 'You don't think there might be a connection?' he asked – 'that heavy work and . . .'

What kind of fools were they?

'For God's sake, why do you think I was frightened? Will you get up at once and ring the doctor. It may be nothing. As you say I may not be pregnant at all, but we can't take any risks for the baby's sake. Don't you realise,' she cried, leaning over and giving him a shake, 'it's the baby that would be harmed – not *me*!' Then, seeing his face take on such a stricken look, she calmed down. 'I honestly am beginning to think,' she said, 'that it *is* a false alarm.'

Two hours later, however, when the doctor had come and gone, Mike ran up the stairs two at a time.

'Well, whatever it was, it was not a false alarm,' he said, trying to make light of it although his face was tight and strained. 'He says there's no need to worry unduly, though. You are to stay in bed, that's all. And he left a prescription for some tablets. Iris is going to town to have it made up. She'll be back as quickly as she can.'

Renée was lying with her two hands down by her sides.

'I don't suppose he means me to lie flat? What do you think? Not all day? I'm sure I can sit up,' she said, starting to do so.

Their roles seemed to have been reversed, though. 'I'd stay flat if I were you,' Mike said tersely. 'You've chanced enough already.' Only she knew him so well, she would have been terribly hurt: his terseness was a form of inverted sympathy.

Then she glanced at the clock, and looked sharply back at him.

'Aren't you going to the office? There isn't any reason to stay home, is there?'

'Oh well, Iris is here anyway,' he said, not noticing he was hedging. He walked over to the window and stood there for a few minutes as if he were looking out, but she felt he was not seeing anything. There was an indefiniteness about him that was uncharacteristic. She watched him nervously. From the window he went to the mantelpiece and fiddled with the clock, and from that he went over to their bookcase and began to read the titles of the books. Like a stranger, she thought. Irritably, she changed the image. No, like a bluebottle! He was annoying her more and more each minute. And then suddenly he came and sat down abruptly on the foot of the bed.

'Renée, how did he establish that you were pregnant – the doctor?'

'He examined me of course – how else?' she said impatiently.

He either did not notice or ignored her annoyance.

'A manual examination?'

She sat up.

'Good heavens, are you crazy?' she asked. It was a matter about which a woman could not afford to be either embarrassed or not embarrassed, but perhaps it was not possible to explain this even to a husband. Suddenly however, Mike's face went to pieces as if he were going to cry.

'Oh Renée, I wish I'd sent for a doctor from Dublin.'

'From Dublin – but why?'

'Oh, I suppose it doesn't matter.' He stood up. There was something on his mind though and next minute he sat down again. 'Oh Renée,' he said miserably, 'it's only that I heard something years ago when we were students. I only heard it by accident but it stuck in my mind. Perhaps I ought not to tell you?'

'Well, you've got to, now you've started – haven't you?' she said coldly. It was hard not to be disturbed.

'Well,' said Mike, 'I was standing in the Main Hall one day, with some medicals.' Renée had to smile in spite of herself at how confidently he launched his worries once he got a hearing, like one of the children, she thought, and her heart softened to him. ' . . . and there was this medical,' he went on. 'He'd just come out from his oral and he was in great form because he'd done pretty well, but he started to tell us about a poor devil that was being examined with him – they take them in pairs – and this other fellow was asked what he'd do if he was called in to establish pregnancy' – he hesitated – 'in a case like yours,' he said, and he hesitated again.

'Go on,' said Renée.

'Well, the first fellow knew the answer himself apparently, because he nearly passed out when he heard the other fellow say he'd examine the woman.'

'But why?' Renée was really alarmed now.

'Well, I only know what the fellow said – that he had to stand there and listen to the poor devil making a fool of himself, knowing what he'd have on his hands in five or six hours – a bloody good haemorrhage.'

Renée was so stunned she could only stare. Miserably, Mike stared back at her.

'I shouldn't have told you,' he said. 'But they were only medical students – *both* of them – maybe the second fellow was right: I never heard the results of that exam!'

Renée wasn't listening. She felt a strange relief. If she were to lose the baby it would not be her fault but the fault of the doctor. She put her hand on Mike's knee and stroked it.

'We'll just have to wait and see, Mike. When I have the tablets they may prevent anything from happening. Go to the office, you: there's no sense in hanging around here all day.'

She felt fine all day and Mike was delighted with how she looked when he got home. Iris and the children had eaten, so he put his own meal on a tray to take it upstairs with Renée. She was in high spirits – when suddenly, without warning she felt her thighs flush uncomfortably. Thinking it was sweat and that she had too many blankets over her, she was leaning forward to throw them back when she realised the sheet was wet: it was . . .

'Mike! Mike!' she screamed. 'Get the doctor.'
It was upon them.

After 'phoning the doctor Mike ran up the stairs and caught her hands and held them.

'Did he say what we should do?' she asked.

'No, just that he'd be here in a few minutes.' He squeezed her hands. Somehow she didn't quite believe him.

'I'm not frightened,' she said.

He turned eagerly. 'Not even if you have to go to the hospital?' he asked, and then he gulped out the rest. 'The doctor said he was arranging for an ambulance.' He stood up. 'What do you think you ought to take with you? I'll get your overnight case.'

'Oh, Mike!' She wasn't frightened, just humiliated. 'You'll come with me in the ambulance, won't you?' she asked, after a minute.

But what was the matter *now*? she wondered. His face had gone white.

'How will the ambulance get in here?' he cried. 'It's been raining all day, the fields will be in a muck. I'd better go down and see if they're coming – down to the road I mean.'

'Raining? I thought there was frost – I'm so cold.' She was shivering. The flow from her body had thinned but it hadn't ceased. And no sooner was Mike gone down the stairs than it came on heavy. Renée exerted all her might and pressed her limbs together. It was impossible to accept that she could not control

K

this flow. The minutes flew past. Mike hadn't packed her case. And where were the children? The house was so silent. She took up her watch from the bedside table but she had forgotten to wind it, and a new panic seized her at not knowing the time. In this panic all sense of time collapsed. Why hadn't Mike come back? Who'd get her down the stairs? The thought of being moved at all terrified her. She felt as if all the blood in her body was seeping out. An odd image came to her mind of ice floes jostling each other down a river in a flood and at the same moment a clot of warm, soft matter left her body.

'Mike. Mike!' she cried out, but it was Iris who ran up the stairs.

'Where did you come from?' Renée asked confused.

'Are you all right?' Iris asked. 'They're having trouble getting the ambulance through the fields: it got stuck a few times and they've had to shovel gravel into the wheel tracks, but don't worry: I think Mike is going to drive it out.'

Then he won't be with me, Renée thought, but she didn't care. A strand of her hair had fallen over her face and she tried to lift her hand to brush it away but her hand seemed to fail and fall back. She tried again. This time she could not raise it at all and the hair felt like something crawling on her skin. For the first time her fear was for herself, not the baby. Am I going to die? she thought. Strangely the thought was translated into words, thin, faint and far far away.

'Hush, hush!' said Iris and *her* voice was so near

and had such a loud rushing sound, Renée wanted to pull away but she couldn't. And why didn't they answer her question? If she was in danger she'd fight; she'd pull herself inward and make a cage of her ribs and stop this leaking away of life.

A strange woman came into the room, followed by a man in uniform, and the next minute Renée was being lifted out of bed. Often in the city she'd seen a stretcher being taken from an ambulance and carried up the steps of a hospital, and she always felt a sinking feeling at the thought of the patient being tilted helplessly on the canvas, but now all that worried her was that her blood would run out faster.

'Oh, where is the ambulance?' she asked, but no one heeded and slowly she began to understand she was already in it and that it was moving.

'I want to talk to my husband,' she said imperatively. No answer. The woman sitting beside her didn't seem to hear.

Then there was another convulsive movement inside her and another mass of some soft pulp passed out of her, and then another.

A dazzling thought came into her mind, although where it came from she could not say. Had she read it? Had someone told it to her? Or was it possible that she was the first to think it? A feeling of great excitement came over her. Was it really possible that she was the first to make so great a discovery – the discovery that, quite simply, one could go on living when one had been emptied of all the things that were supposed to matter, lungs, liver, kidney, heart. For of course those blobs and clots that had flowed out of her – those ice floes! – remember – remember – those were her liver, her kidneys, her lungs, her heart. And yet she was still living.

She was cleaned-out as she'd often herself cleaned out a fowl, and yet she was alive! If only she could get up she could move and walk about; could *run*. She would be so light that like a bird she might be able to fly. What an amazing discovery to make just by intuition alone. But that was the way Newton had discovered gravity – oh, she'd have to tell someone oh, but not this stupid nurse. And anyway she was tired, so tired. First she must sleep.

I am still alive, Renée thought, when, without opening her eyes she heard voices talking, yes, and calling her name, but they were very far away, on the shore perhaps, while she was still detained in a cold mist-filled sea.

Struggling to wade ashore, she suddenly felt Mike's warm hands clasping hers and – did she dare? – she opened her eyes.

What an absurd dream, she thought. She was in a bright and sunny room, filled with flowers, and Mike was bending over her.

'Oh Mike!'

'Oh Renée.' He pressed her hands. 'Oh Renée! Thank God: thank God. I was so frightened.'

But why? She couldn't understand. She was so

happy; so comfortable, a bit sleepy but then she'd just wakened up.

'What time is it?' she asked.

Mike was looking at her as if he could never get his fill of her.

'Oh Renée,' he whispered. 'They said you were in no real danger but I was scared – you were so weak and you kept asking if you were dying.'

'Dying?' She laughed. Then she remembered the baby. 'Oh Mike. Did I lose it?' she cried.

Mike hesitated a minute. 'Bother the baby,' he said, then quickly: 'It was you that mattered.'

Sobered, the tears rushed into Renée's eyes and her joy in the sunlight and the flowers faded.

'Why wasn't I more careful?' she said.

'It wasn't your carelessness,' said Mike. 'That God damn fool of a doctor –'

'There would have been no need of him if I had acted right,' she said. Then, in a loud voice, not caring that the nurse had come back, 'I killed our baby,' she said, and began to cry.

'Oh come now,' said the nurse, but she addressed herself mainly to Mike. 'It's only to be expected,' she said. 'I think we should let her rest now: she'll feel better later.'

Did she feel better when she woke again? At least she felt like sitting up and she readily put her arms into the sleeves of the flowery bedjacket the nurse held out for her.

'A present from your sister,' said the young nurse.
Immediately the tears rushed into Renée's eyes.

'It's not an occasion for celebration,' she said,
although Mike was just coming around the door with
more flowers.

'Well, we feel like celebrating,' said Mike and he
bent and kissed her with a tenderness that nearly made
her heart break. 'I know how you feel about the baby,'
he said. Then suddenly he made a funny face, 'but
there are plenty more where that one came from.'

She pushed him away because of the nurse. 'You're
messing up the bed,' she said. 'Sit down at the
end.'

But the nurse had heard what Mike said and she
was delighted.

'We'll have you back with us within the year,' she
said to Renée. 'How many will that be you'll have –
children I mean?'

Renée was given a jolt.

'Isn't that odd?' she said, turning back to Mike. 'I'd
forgotten the children. I never once thought of them,
even when I felt I might be dying. I didn't even think of
you, Mike.' But in case he was hurt she put her hand
on his arm. 'What did you feel?' she asked. 'When you
knew I was in danger – what was your first thought?'

Mike's face, so strained up to that, became really
normal for the first time in twenty-four hours.

'Do you really want to know what I thought?' he
said boyishly. 'Well, the first thing I thought was that
the farm was in your name. That's honest, Renée. I

know it sounds awful, but it's *honest*. Of course a minute after – '

'Don't explain.' She took his hand. 'I know exactly how it was. I'm so glad you told me. That is the reality of our life together, isn't it – of our marriage? We are truthful with each other always, no matter what. And it was the proper thing for you to feel because, if I had died, it would have been you who'd have to do everything alone, rear the children and educate them. . . .' But she interrupted herself. '*That* is why *I* didn't think of you and the children of course – I knew where you were, but it was me that was going into the unknown. And the poor baby. That's why I had all those queer dreams too. I didn't tell you but I had terrible dreams.' She sat up and pushed back her hair. 'And just a few minutes ago – before you came in – I had such a very strange one. I was at home and there were men digging a hole under the big elm tree on the lawn, the one with the crocuses under it, and when I went over to see what they were doing I saw a little baby, naked, lying on the grass. I didn't know they were going to put it in the hole because I thought it was alive, but when they'd dug deep enough they went to lift the baby and then I knew. I tried to cry out and stop them but no sound came – you know how that happens in a dream but they weren't able to lift the baby. They kept trying and trying but they couldn't and then I realised the baby wasn't made of flesh and blood at all, because I could see through it. It was like a soap bubble – only it was alive. I saw the grass through it, and the crocuses. I know it sounds silly, but I was happy because I knew then they couldn't put it in the clay. I thought it might even float away into the sky – I woke up then. But oh Mike, why can't – '

Mike bent down and went to kiss her.

'Oh my darling,' he said.

Renée submitted for a minute to the happiness of being loved. Then uneasily her mind strayed back to what she had been trying to say. 'That's why I feel bad about our baby. Where is it now? Or had it not begun to live? What do you think, Mike?'

Mike had lost his bearings, though. He looked to the nurse for help. She came over.

'We must not over-do things the first few days,' she said to Renée. 'Easy does it. That's the idea. You may feel well, but I bet you wouldn't like to be asked to run a mile!' She turned and reassured Mike. 'She'll be as gay as a lark by the time she's ready to go home!'

Only it wasn't so: it wasn't so at all. As the days passed Renée got more depressed, not less. And when he came to see her Mike was no longer happy or loving. He didn't bring the children to see her either: not once.

'What is the matter, Renée?' he asked miserably on the day before she was due to go home.

'I don't know,' she said. 'I just keep thinking of the baby.'

'I see,' he said shortly, and he left after a few minutes.

That evening when she wasn't expecting any visitors he walked into the room.

'Guess who's coming to see you tonight?' he said. 'It was Iris who thought of it. She's bringing him in her car – Father Hugh. He's going to talk to you about that business – it's that that's on your mind isn't it – the thing we talked about in Achill?'

She stared at him, first in amazement, then in dismay.

'Oh, I'd forgotten about that,' she cried, and she put her hand to her forehead. 'Oh, that makes it worse,' she said, almost in a moan.

She was sobbing when Iris and Father Hugh arrived. Mike confronted them at the door.

'She says it wasn't that at all,' he said accusingly to Iris.

Iris walked past him and went straight over to the bed.

'Here's Father Hugh, Renée,' she said. 'Aren't you glad to see him – no matter what?'

Mike intervened. 'What does that mean?' he demanded.

Father Hugh gently put him aside.

'I hear you are worried about your little baby's soul, Renée,' he said levelly. 'But you know God's love is infinite, don't you, and our poor minds. . . .' As she stared coldly at him his tone changed. 'Would it make you happier if I told you there is a growing body of opinion in the Church to the effect that the Vatican may be prepared to admit to error in its theories of Limbo – it was never a dogma, you know.'

But when Renée turned away her head, Father Hugh turned to Mike.

'Who was her doctor?' he asked. 'Was he a Catholic? Some of them are very scrupulous and have been known – '

But suddenly Iris raised her voice.

'Please!' she said. 'She was only a few weeks pregnant! And I've heard of those medical baptists and what I heard turned my stomach.'

Shocked by her tone and the vehemence of her words, Father Hugh looked at her.

'Iris?' he said, astonished, 'I thought you brought me here because . . .'

Iris stared unflinchingly at him.

'Well, you thought wrong,' she said. 'What more does the Church know than any of us in this matter – or in fact' – but beyond this she didn't go, her face cold and proud.

Speechless, Renée stared at her and then she stretched out her hand which Iris immediately took and fiercely held.

'Iris is right,' Renée said. 'If it's anyone's guess why shouldn't it be mine – or at least a woman's? Why does it have to be so complicated and involved.' She turned to Mike. 'Tell him my dream,' she commanded.

To her surprise Mike's face was dark with annoyance.

'Look here, Renée,' he said. 'You're not thinking – just because of this – of giving up your religion, are you? Not when you've only just embraced it! It would have been better if you had never turned. What will people say? What will I tell the children?'

Father Hugh put a hand on his shoulder.

'Stop shouting at her, Mike,' he said. 'If it didn't take, it didn't take.'

Iris gave a sudden laugh. 'You make it seem like a pock,' she said, but she was serious again immediately. 'Anyway it's not her faith in God that is in question, is it?' she said and she turned to Renée. 'But you can see why I didn't want you to rush into a religion that makes everything so hard – so *impossibly* hard.' She looked back at Father Hugh. 'God couldn't want that, could He?'

But Father Hugh was looking very strangely at her.

'I'll tell you what we'll do,' he said, 'when our patient comes home and has built up her strength – we'll have it all out – the three of us' – but here he pulled himself up – 'and you too, of course, Mike,' he said. 'We'll talk this whole thing over calmly.'

'And truthfully!' Iris stabbed, 'with no false loyalties. . . .'

Father Hugh laughed. 'No holds barred!' he said.

Iris smiled. Never, never, since they were girls had Renée seen her look so pretty – beautiful really – she thought with surprise. She herself was forgotten, it seemed, but it was extraordinary how at peace she felt. All that was wanted from her anyway was that she get well and strong again.

Poor Mike! she thought: They all seemed to have

shut him out – but not deliberately because, no matter what Iris may have thought, she and Mike had grown very close. She caught his hand. She wanted to reassure him; to restore him to his usual good form. But she was getting sleepy again; not weak, nor as if she was losing consciousness, just sleepy. Maybe in the beginning she and Mike weren't exactly two of a kind but –

Her eyes flew open. Was *that* what Iris meant that day. . . ? She'd have to ask her. But when she looked at her, Iris was looking at Father Hugh.

'You're a man after my own heart, Iris,' Father Hugh said, and this Iris found so funny she laughed. Father Hugh laughed too. Really Iris looked very beautiful. I must tell her so, Renée thought happily. But she couldn't keep her eyes open another instant. As they fell shut everything in the room was transfixed in light, Mike and the nurse and the masses of flowers – and Iris and Father Hugh still looking at each other.